Black Cloud, White Cloud

AUTHOR AND ARTIST SERIES

By Ellen Douglas

A Family's Affairs
Black Cloud, White Cloud
Where the Dreams Cross
Apostles of Light
The Rock Cried Out
A Lifetime Burning
The Magic Carpet and Other Tales
Can't Quit You, Baby

Black Cloud, White Cloud

by Ellen Douglas

Illustrated by Elizabeth Wolfe

UNIVERSITY PRESS OF MISSISSIPPI

JACKSON AND LONDON

AUTHOR AND ARTIST SERIES

Morgana: Two Stories from 'The Golden Apples'
by Eudora Welty, with illustrations by
Mildred Nungester Wolfe

Library of Congress Cataloging-in-Publication Data

Douglas, Ellen, 1921–
    Black cloud, white cloud / by Ellen Douglas : illustrated
by Elizabeth Wolfe.
        p.   cm. — (Author and artist series)
    Revision of the original ed. : New York : Houghton
Mifflin, 1963.
    ISBN 0-87805-393-X.
    ISBN 0-87805-397-2 (special limited ed.)
    1. Mississippi—Fiction. I. Title. II. Series.
PS3554.O825B58   1989   89-5524
813'.54—dc19   CIP

The Little Black Boy

My mother bore me in the southern wild,
    And I am black, but O, my soul is white!
White as an angel is the English child,
    But I am black, as if bereav'd of light.

My mother taught me underneath a tree,
    And, sitting down before the heat of day,
She took me on her lap and kissèd me,
    And, pointing to the East, began to say:

"Look on the rising sun: there God does live,
    And gives His light, and gives His heat away,
And flowers and trees and beasts and men receive
    Comfort in morning, joy in the noonday.

"And we are put on earth a little space,
    That we may learn to bear the beams of love;
And these black bodies and this sunburnt face
    Are but a cloud, and like a shady grove.

"For when our souls have learn'd the heat to bear,
    The cloud will vanish; we shall hear His voice,
Saying, 'Come out from the grove, my love and care,
    And round my golden tent like lambs rejoice.'"

Thus did my mother say, and kissèd me,
    And thus I say to little English boy.
When I from black and he from white cloud free,
    And round the tent of God, like lambs we joy,

I'll shade him from the heat till he can bear
    To lean in joy upon our Father's knee;
And then I'll stand and stroke his silver hair,
    And be like him, and he will then love me.

                        William Blake

The House on the Bluff
(Homochitto)

I

B E H I N D the Baird house in Homochitto a double garçonnière encloses a brick-paved court, and behind the garçonnière a carefully tended lawn slopes away to the old carriage house, servants' quarters, and vegetable garden. Around two sides and the back a brick wall, grown with intricate patterns of fig vine and sprinkled with shards of broken glass to discourage intruders, cuts off the view of the Negro slum that rolls up on every hand in a confusion of patched and slanting roofs and half-dead chinaberry trees. A city block is encompassed by the wall, a self-contained world looking out across Baird Heights Drive to a narrow clipped park perched on top of the shale bluff that drops two hundred feet to the river—the slow brown Mississippi, pouring along its mud-heavy tide.

The house—two stories with long galleries across the front, upstairs and down—faces the river; from the upstairs gallery one can see for miles across the flat Louisiana farm land on the other side. Here, as the family was once told by an artist who stayed with them for weeks while painting Margaret Baird's portrait, one can watch every evening the most beautiful sunsets in the world.

"The water turns to blood," he said, "the heavens are all light,

and the clouds afire. You might imagine yourself inside a furnace."
So he described it, in the high-flown language that painters from
New Orleans sometimes use. But he may have meant only to flatter
them regarding a view which he knew they felt belonged especially
to them.

Seventy years ago half a dozen mansions enjoyed the view across
the river, but with the passage of time the neighborhood has
changed. A landslide, following torrential spring rains one year in
the late nineties, carried away a slice of the park and threatened the
whole area; the owners one by one sold out and moved back from
the bluff. Now, of the six big houses two have burned, one stands
shuttered and deserted by heirs who have moved to New York City,
one is occupied by the standard, eccentric, alcoholic tag end of a
dead line, and the oldest, dating from Homochitto's Spanish period,
is a Negro tenement.

Not far off, within walking distance through the slum, is a more
respectable residential neighborhood. Here, in another tall isolated
house surrounded by gardens and outbuildings, old Mrs. McGovern
and her maiden sister, Celestine, used to live; and it was here, in the
nineteen twenties and thirties, that Anna McGovern and her family
came every year for a summer visit.

The Bairds and McGoverns are joined by all the complicated
strands of kinship, love, and enmity that bind together families who
have lived cheek by jowl in a small town for five or six generations.
Cousins have married cousins until no one can say with certainty
how the latest generations are connected. Margaret Baird and
Charlotte McGovern sometimes jokingly told their daughters, Caroline and Anna, that they were sixth cousins on one side and half-
fourth cousins on the other. This of course did not take into account

the common in-laws who had married each other from time to time for a hundred and fifty years.

Anna and Caroline were friends. Their mothers, friends from childhood, had been married the same year, and the two children had been born the same summer. They had learned to walk and talk together, and had grown up playing every summer side by side, as it were, but scarcely *with* each other, each one occupied with her own imaginings. Later, when Anna was eight or nine, they began to write to each other, in the winter, long letters about their adventures. Anna was a warrior in the retinue of Genghis Khan, and wrote of forays against the Great Wall, marches into India and Persia, bloody massacres, captured cities, and coffers of pearls; Caroline, an orphan princess held captive by the Saracens, wrote that the Maharajah of Shodipur was raising her ransom by a levy on the richest and most powerful of his subjects. It was her idea that they should write their letters from right to left and from the bottom of the page up.

Then, summer: the first thing Anna did, after kissing her grandmother and great-aunt, was to race out of the back gate, skip and run the seven blocks to the Baird house, and let herself in through the heavy carriage-house door. Here, too, was an imagined land, a place set off. Out of the hot June day, through the cool darkness of the carriage house, overhung by deep shade, its doorway grown around like the entrance to a cave with wisteria vines as thick as a man's thigh, its walls breathing a marvelous smell of damp mossy brick, and then out again into the green sun-dappled gloom of the courtyard between the galleries of the garçonnières.

For nearly twenty years the Baird house was a home away from home for Anna—a world as complex as her own, but different, that made her welcome without question and revealed itself slowly, unconsciously, taking her in and forcing her in return to say welcome to it. It was a world with concrete attractions for a child: chests of games, marionettes and hand puppets, dollhouses taller than a child's head, electric trains, tanks of goldfish, swings, and a double trapeze cluttered the galleries and court of the garçonnières, and the yard was overrun with dogs, cats, and pet ducks. There was even a Shetland pony.

It follows that by Homochitto's modest standards the Bairds were wealthy. Caroline's father, Keith Baird, dead by the time she was four, had been the second son of a prosperous Massachusetts textile family with longtime cotton interests and family connections in Mississippi. Sent South shortly before the First World War to look after the family holdings, he had met and married his distant cousin, Margaret Baird, and had stayed on. He had bought the Baird house from Margaret's childless aunt and uncle, had rescued it at a moment when it seemed ready to slide down the bluff and into the river, and turned it into the showplace of the town.

People who knew them both say that Keith, with his openhearted charm and classic good looks, reminded them of Scott Fitzgerald. He had the same straight nose and small, beautifully chiseled mouth, weak, but ingratiating. With money, social position, and intelligence, Keith was the catch of his "crowd." His cousin Margaret, slender and dark, with a coquettish smile and slanting green eyes, was the belle of hers. After a few months of being wooed away from her girlish reluctance, she caught him.

With everything to live for, Keith died of a heart attack at thirty-six. Fortunately, he left his young family considerable local rental property, some farmland, and a block of stock in the Homochitto Bank and Trust Company, as well as an interest in the family mills.

Margaret did not remarry. Only thirty when he died, she began, after a suitable period of mourning, to have too good a time.

And so it happened that by the time Anna McGovern was old enough to look around her, the Baird house was one of the gayest places between Memphis and New Orleans. It was a formal gaiety—presided over with iron discipline by the Negro woman, Tété, who had been Margaret's mother's maid, her own nurse, and was now her children's second mother—a perfectly ordered life where breakfast was served to guests in their rooms, where maids in crisp uniforms went about their duties on silent feet, and a uniformed chauffeur was available if one wished to take a ride. Dinner, at four o'clock in accordance with old-fashioned Southern custom, was never for less than eight or ten: Margaret and her son Keith, Caroline, the children's guests, house guests, and usually a friend or two of Margaret's who had "dropped in."

Uncritically, in truth joyfully and even worshipfully, Anna took it all in. Once or twice her mother warned her that she must guard herself against being envious of Keith and Caroline, that she must make up her mind "for good and all" to accept the fact that they would always have more than she did. Anna listened and nodded and felt quite virtuous (she was a serious-minded child who seldom resisted the temptation to feel virtuous) because she was not envious. She did not inquire of herself why, or stop to consider that if one simply, without effort, is *not*, there can't be much credit attached to the lack. When she was older, she would recognize that her parents had given her so strong a sense of the reality of her own life, her own place in the world, embedded like a pebble in a piece of pudding stone, that she could not have been envious. The emotion would have presupposed a kind of failure of which they knew nothing.

To other strictures from her mother and aunts on the subject of the Baird family, Anna, round-faced and earnest, listened with equally uncritical interest, as she listened to everything that grown people said, storing away like a magpie the data of her experience—diamonds, rhinestones, and dimestore rings—in a glittering jumble at the bottom of her mind.

She heard them speak with mild disapproval of Tété's position in the family. They would never have permitted a servant—a "colored person"—no matter how devoted, how competent, to raise *their* children. Servants, even devoted servants, were one thing; but to turn over one's *family*, to relinquish all responsibility, as they believed Margaret Baird had, that was another matter.

Charlotte, who sometimes *had* to speak her mind, whose face in any case, as she often said herself with an incomprehensible pride in her peculiar failings, was always a dead giveaway, even told Margaret what she thought about it, and afterwards with considerable satisfaction repeated the conversation to her sisters.

"I feel sorry for you, Charlotte," Margaret had said. "I feel sorry for anyone who doesn't have a Tété. Now, you see" (This had been on an occasion when Charlotte could not take a long-looked-forward-to trip with her husband because her mother, who had promised to keep the children, was sick, and his mother out of town), "if you were me, you wouldn't have any problem. I can go where I please and stay as long as I please and always be sure the children and the house are all right. In fact," she had shrugged, "I believe Tété manages better when I'm not here."

"You needn't feel sorry for me, my dear," Charlotte had said. "I wouldn't want to leave my children in the care of a Negro for two whole weeks."

"A Negro!" Margaret had said. "I'm talking about Tété."

"With all due respect to Tété," Charlotte had said, "I'd rather raise my family myself."

"Well!" Margaret had said. "I think that's almost . . . *common*."

Of course they were cousins—almost like sisters. They felt free to say what they liked to each other. In a day or two the conversation had been forgotten by everyone except Anna, who had taken it in with a swell of pride. *Her* mother preferred to raise her own children. She wouldn't leave them with a Negro, not even Tété.

On another occasion she heard a grown-up cousin whisper to her mother the gossip that Tété used a horsewhip on Keith Baird when he misbehaved.

"A horsewhip! Well, I don't believe *that*!"

"I've heard it's absolutely true. Louise Baird says . . ."

"You know Louise Baird is the biggest liar in Homochitto," Charlotte said. She looked thoughtful. "And besides," she added, "Keith is getting out of hand, Lord knows. He probably needs it. Just last week I heard that he and Billy Stanton were caught climbing out onto the courthouse cupola to catch pigeons."

"But . . ."

"Yes, I know. It's *shocking*. I wonder if Margaret knows . . . *If it's true, I mean.*"

"Oh, she gives Tété a free hand. Whatever Tété says goes."

This tag of gossip about the horsewhip Anna took in with interest and turned over dispassionately in her mind. What does it look like, she thought, and visualized to herself not a quirt or even a buggy whip, but an eight-foot plaited leather lash with a short heavy stock like the ones the covered-wagon drivers used in the Saturday cowboy movies. And then: I wonder where she keeps it. I've never seen it. She kept her eyes open for the horsewhip all that summer, even getting a glimpse one day, when she had been sent to get out the checkers game, into Tété's closet. She saw the checkerboard and the box of men on a shelf to her left where she had only to take them up without touching anything else; but hastily, half-sick with guilt and daring, she pushed aside Tété's long dark dresses, hoping to see the whip (perhaps stained brown with human blood?) hidden at the back of the closet. She found nothing but an old umbrella with a broken handle.

It mattered not at all to Anna that she spent two or three weeks every year with the Bairds and, when she was not staying there, played every summer day with Caroline, and that she had never heard Tété raise her voice to the children, much less seen her take a whip to them. It was no feat for her to accept everything she heard a grown person say as true, and at the same time to accept the evidence of her own senses that it was not true. The world, after all, was at best confusing, and Tété's place in it was only one of its many puzzling phenomena.

Looking back as a grown woman, Anna could not remember when she had first known Tété, any more than she could remember "meeting" the Bairds; but she could see Tété as she was then, far more vividly than she saw her own mother at the same period, or even herself. Her first memory came from the year she was five, and spending the night away from home for the first time in her life.

It was early morning and she was awake, waiting for someone to tell her she could get up. The door opened and Tété came into the darkened room, a short, almost dwarfish, but strongly-built, dark brown woman, wearing the ankle-length full skirt and many petticoats of an earlier generation, a bibbed white apron dropping to the hemline. So she dressed then, and so she continued to dress until she died, conceding, as the years passed, perhaps two inches of skirt to the demands of changing fashion. She walked with a heavy jarring tread, coming down on each foot as thumpingly as if that leg were shorter than the other, her body and skirts swaying jerkily from side to side. She set a breakfast tray on a table, went to the windows, drew back the curtains to let in the morning sun, then picked up the tray set with spotless linen and shining silver, and brought it to Anna's beside.

"Good morning, Anna," she said. "Here's your breakfast. Sit up now and put a pillow on your lap for the tray. There."

Anna, who had never had breakfast in bed except when she was ill, was delighted, her pleasure only slightly dimmed by the observation that there was no jelly to put on the hot biscuits.

Tété went out and returned with a tray for Caroline. There were no admonitions about spilling, no instructions about eating a good breakfast, no conversation except for the exchange of good mornings. Tété was not one to waste words, nor did she ever condescend. She came, did what had to be done, and left. Her manner said, "You have your ways and I have mine, but I know we are equals; I won't take advantage of you."

A child so seldom senses justice in a grown person that he cannot forget it.

Anna's other early memory, probably from the same year, was of a birthday party for Caroline. Other parties during her childhood she remembered afterwards with vague discomfort: the boring ordeal of pinning the tail on the donkey or pushing a pea around the floor with her nose, the games of drop-the-handkerchief and going-to-Jerusalem, during which, even as a small child, she felt that she was being made a fool of. But Caroline's party!

The air was full of bubbles—gold and emerald and sapphire blue, bigger than a child's head, tied in clusters and tugging at their

strings, drifting like schools of queer, round, translucent fish along the ceiling of the gallery, nosing at the screens and bumping gently at the doors and windows. Someone gave her one, and she raced out into the court with it. The string slipped from her hand and it sailed away, up into the sky, until it vanished. Her heart was so filled with emotion—joy for its flight, sorrow for her loss—that she flapped her arms and spun around until she dropped, dizzy, to the ground.

Dozens of children seemed to be dancing about her, as the party cartwheeled above her head; to recover herself, she stared in concentration at the buttons on her new Roman sandals, counting them and then counting them again. Then she stood up slowly, ready to burst into hysterical tears. But she knew something else was going to happen, some secret was to be revealed, and she composed herself to wait and watch for it.

One of the storerooms in the garçonnière had been turned into a kind of dim, candlelit, mosquito-netting-draped grotto and, after lemonade and tea cakes, the children were told that a fairy lived in this cave, a winged fairy who could really fly and who was so fond of children that she had a present for each of them.

Anna, always a gullible child willing to believe in any mystery for as long as grown people would allow her to, went into the lovely dimness with awe and pleasure, and there, seeming to her dazzled eyes to be floating inches above the floors, was a tall, white-robed creature with a veil over her face and a soft cooing voice, who called her by name and gave her a small golden box. She rushed to her mother.

"Mama! The fairy knew me! She knew my name!"

At the same time she was aware, as a separate fact, that the cooing voice should be attached to a grown-up cousin whose saccharine smile and passion for hugging children made her uneasy.

"She did!" Charlotte said. "And what did she give you? Let's see what's in your box."

Just then Anna caught sight of Tété, who was keeping order among the excited children outside the fairy's grotto. Tété was looking straight at her. The short, dark, deeply lined face with its strong flat nose had on it a look of concentrated disdain. The pendulous lower lip was thrust out, the small body rigidly erect, the black eyes bright as a hungry bird's. For an instant Anna imagined that Tété might take a pin from the shoulder strap of her apron and pop every balloon. This glimpse of a violent, a virulently passionate emotion, lasted only an instant and was replaced by something less frightening. Tété, after all, was a grown person, and a special kind of grown person—one who could always be trusted to be herself. This make-believe was foolishness to her; she had dissociated herself from it and did not hesitate to let Anna see her contempt for it. Anna turned her back and, crowding close against her mother's knees, opened the present that the fairy had given her.

For weeks after the party, wandering occasionally through the courtyard, Anna would glance hastily around to see if anyone was watching, and then would peep into the fairy's abandoned home, still draped with dusty mosquito bars; she half hoped to see again the white figure with tinseled wings, floating in the empty, silent air. But, at the same time, she remembered the familiarity of the fairy's cooing voice and, afterwards, Tété's face.

II

AT THAT TIME, during the nineteen twenties and thirties, the
little town of Homochitto, under the shade of its old trees, cut into
queer sections by the deep ravines of wandering bayous where at
night one could sometimes hear the bobcats scream, seemed no more
than a temporary bastion against the surrounding wilderness. It had
been sixty years and more since the Civil War had swept away the
brief generation of its grandeur, and now the woods encroached
everywhere around the Georgian and Louisiana colonial houses
whose gardens were tangles of grapevines, thickets of Spanish dag-
gers and green thorny mock orange plants, drifted in late spring with
a snow of delicate flowerets.

Keith and Caroline and Anna, in spite of their orderly lives
within the confines of the walls that surrounded the Baird house and
the old McGovern place, felt themselves to be wilderness children.
They grew up in tangled gardens, built their retreats under the
branches of magnolia trees that swept the ground on every side, rode
and walked the deep shale cuts overhung with clusters of wild
hydrangea blossoms shining in the gloom, and saw in imagination
the tracks of Indians, bison, bear, and deer that over hundreds, thou-

sands of years had worn the trails along which the roads into Homochitto wound.

Keith, who was used to wandering the countryside alone and knew every footpath and county road for miles around, would point out the wild birds and name them for the little girls: kingfishers and green herons banking and dipping over sunny pasture ponds, cardinals, yellow-breasted field larks, and mourning doves, gray as a foggy morning. Occasionally, so rarely that they talked about it for days afterwards, they would see a painted bunting, all green and red and iridescent blue, exotic as a parrot, flash for a moment in the summer air, and vanish into a tangled cherokee rose hedge or blackberry thicket.

When Clarence, the Bairds' chauffeur, brought the children's horses in from the country, they could ride out through the gate behind the carriage house, northward along a road that followed the curving course of the river, and within half a mile of the house turn off on a wagon track where they might start up a covey of quail that filled the air with the machine-gun rattle of its flight and sent the horses shying into the weedy ditches, or follow a footpath through the woods to the places where the wild muscadine and scuppernong vines grew. To Anna particularly, since she did not live in Homochitto and so was not tricked into blindness by the boredom of rainy winter Saturdays or the dull repetitions of routine, the Baird household—walls sprinkled with shards of glass, clipped gardens, and shining silverware—seemed more itself because the wilderness was all around; because in a queer, perpendicular way, climbing the face of the bluff that dropped to the river on the other side of Baird Heights Drive, the forest grew up to the very door.

The bluff was a forest forbidden to the children. They were not allowed to climb the low fence that ran along its edge, even to look down into the tops of the trees growing from its face. But in the country, when they drove out to visit one or another of the friends and cousins who lived on the poor hill-farms around Homochitto that were grandly called "plantations," and particularly on Saturday when sometimes they went with Tété to spend the day at her sister Selina's place a mile or two north of the town, they were free to roam.

Here, too, they found on the one hand order and sunshine—neat white cottage, straight rows of cotton, fenced-in pasture and horse lot—and on the other the gray moss-bearded wood. Sitting on the porch of Selina's house, they could hear from the wood the mourning dove's call, three soft questioning notes, full of sorrow, far away; and then, nearer, the answer, the drawn-out breath of a grieving ghost. Keith, green-eyed and curly-haired like his mother, a dark and solitary Pan, sat on the steps in the late afternoon and blew the same three notes on a battered clay ocarina—his "sweet potato." But from the south side of the house, far up in the sky over the pasture, they heard the field lark's whistle, high and piercing, unbelievably sweet, the very joy of summer. Keith could not make the soft-voiced ocarina mock those notes.

Although Anna was scarcely conscious of the lark and the doves when as a child she spent so many Saturdays in the country, and although afterwards she heard the same calls in the fields and forests of other places, the two sounds together never afterwards failed to bring her up short: the neat little house, the woods and bayou, the green fields—Selina's farm. And with that thought, an aching discomfort—was it joy or pain? Then, in resolution, a tumble of images: the white gander craning his neck, stretching his wings, and hissing by the pond, an arrowhead stumbled on in a furrow of the cornfield between pasture and bayou, a wild ride on the horses, icy water riffling over her feet as they waded in the bayou. Yes, she would reassure herself, we had good times. We were lucky. And then, as if the dove were calling, *But Keith, Keith, Keith?* And the lark in reply, *Caro-, Caroline.*

For Anna, the collapse of her childhood vision of the Baird household—the fairyland world of ceremonious and exotic charm—happened one summer weekend in 1931. It was not so much that anything changed that weekend, for even Tété's fall changed nothing, as that Anna, like a skater on cracking ice, saw the surface of the Bairds' life broken and for a moment glimpsed unimagined and threatening depths. Baffled by all that happened, Anna was silent, but later she remembered. Clearly things had been thus and so, and if one chose to consider the events with attention and intelligence, at least some of the reasons were available.

Anna and Caroline were ten that summer, old enough to know that times were changing, that, although they might be shielded from it, some upheaval was taking place in the outside world. The Bairds' textile mills had already failed. True, there was still considerable rental property, a small farm, and stock in the local bank to fall back on, but the annual trip to the mountains had been canceled. At the dinner table the children occasionally heard talk to which they paid no attention about the stock market, bankruptcy, and the presidential election. Margaret's own parents and her father- and mother-in-law were all dead now, and she had to be head of her family. Everyone noticed that summer that she got perceptibly heavier—almost as if she were storing strength and weight for the future. She had always been what the women's magazines call "willowy"—a slender, springing shaft of a woman, all grace and motion. Now she began to be, instead of willowy, "stately." She was tall and carried the weight easily; she lost none of the sexual magic that had kept her surrounded by men since she was twelve—the curly smile and provocative green eyes continued automatically, no matter what problem her mind might be occupied with, to play the games of courtship. She always had a "beau." And she always had female friends, too. Generous without thought, she was as generous with her charm as with her possessions. She had never been in a situation (except the girlhood one, common to all self-respecting Southern girls, of stealing beaux) where she had to be ruthless, and so no one, least of all herself, had taken her measure. Tété perhaps had, who had known her so long and well, but no one else except her children, Keith and Caroline, who did not of course *know* their mother, but grew in their silent way in her shadow.

Margaret and her current beau, a wealthy widower from Baton Rouge, were to go to New Orleans that June weekend, on the kind of shopping and eating trip that people from Homochitto periodically made. It was Friday morning, a soft green day, almost springlike. The Bairds' car (not the black Cadillac limousine with jump seats that took the children to Sunday school, but a pale blue Buick with a narrow cream-colored stripe around the body just above the door handles) was drawn up at the front gate, the chauffeur lounging against the fender in a spot of shade.

Anna and Caroline were waiting in the front yard to say goodbye. For an hour they had been playing an absorbing game on the brick walk under the low branches of the laurel tree, making patterns of melted wax with lighted candles, dripping the hot wax in wavering lines on the bricks and on their own hands and arms. Caroline's long, straight, brown hair fell forward over her thin shoulders; her face already had the tragic intensity and slight distortion of early adolescence, the nose and teeth a trifle too large, the mouth unfinished, as it were. She would never be so beautiful as her mother, and now, growing up too soon and too fast, she was at her worst. She was making the outline of a cat on the bricks with drops of yellow wax. Anna, her fine blonde hair stringing down in uneven lengths from a crooked part, a smudge of dirt across her wide flat-tish nose, legs and arms pocked with mosquito bites, was writing her name on her arm.

From inside the house Tété called for the chauffeur to come and get the suitcases. At the sound of her voice, Caroline jumped up.

"Come on, come on," she whispered urgently to Anna. "Quick."

"Huh?" Anna looked up absently from her work. "Wait a minute. I'm not through."

Caroline stooped and blew out her candle.

"Hey, quit it. Hey . . ."

"Hurry," Caroline said again, and began to dance up and down and flap her long arms with a wild awkward gaiety. "Let's play a trick on Margaret." (The two children called their mother Margaret; Tété still called her by a childhood nickname, "Sweet.") "Come on," Caroline said. "Don't ask questions, just come on."

They climbed through the tangle of closely grown branches, all sticky with oozing sap, until they were high up in the laurel tree, hidden from the ground by masses of foliage, and, perched there, peered out through an opening between the branches and saw Margaret and the beau, Keith, Tété, and the chauffeur come out of the house. There were last-minute instructions, a hug for Tété, and a peck on the cheek for Keith, who at thirteen considered himself too old to be embraced by his mother. Then they looked around for Caroline. Clarence was sent to search for her. Margaret stood in the shade of the laurel tree, cool and lovely in a green linen dress the color of her eyes. She shrugged her shoulders impatiently and lit a cigarette. Anna whispered to Caroline in growing alarm that they had better climb down. But Caroline shook her head stubbornly, her face in the green gloom full of a queer crafty joy. What could she have expected? Anna did not know. She knew only that she felt uneasy and guilty.

After five minutes' delay, Margaret called off the search. "They're around somewhere," she said. "They must have forgotten we were leaving. We'd better go on. Bill and Louise are waiting for us."

They drove away in the long, blue Buick, waving and laughing, looking as if they might be an advertisement for the car. Tété and Keith went into the house. Clarence lingered a few minutes by the gate and then wandered off toward the back yard. In the tree, Caroline began to weep.

"What's the matter?" Anna said. And then, when she got no answer, "Don't cry, Caroline. It's all right. Don't cry." And finally, "For Pete's sake, it was your idea, after all."

"Oh, shut up, will you!" Caroline said. "You're just *dumb.* That's all that's the matter with you. You're *dumb.*"

Anna climbed down from the tree with slow dignity, lighted a candle, and began with affected absorption to make wax patterns on the bricks. She and Caroline did not speak to each other for fifteen minutes. Then Caroline, scrambling out of the tree, began a conversation as cheerfully as if nothing had happened, with only an occasional sniff or sobbing gasp of breath to betray her grief. Within a few minutes they had decided to play Indian and papoose.

They slipped quietly into the nursery, found a couple of dolls, and spent the rest of the morning in the park across the street, constructing bark and twine cradle boards for the papooses. When these were finished, they climbed the low picket fence that ran along about three feet back from the edge of the bluff, and, standing on tiptoes, hung their babies in a little tree that grew up from the face of the bluff below them. Then, having already disobeyed the house rule against climbing the fence and so having nothing more to lose, they lay on their stomachs and peered downward into the thicket of brambles and small trees that grew out of the face of the bluff.

Just north of where they lay, the bluff, following the curve of the river, swung to the westward, and they could see its face for some hundreds of yards before it bent back on itself. The green of the tangled growth was broken here and there by a narrow path of brown where a small slide had covered or carried down the shallow-rooted brambles and small trees to a pile at the foot of the bluff.

Anna inched forward to see more of the area directly below them; and a shower of dust and dirt clods rained down through the weeds and thickets onto a narrow slanting shale ledge. "Look there," she said. "See that ledge? There's a hole right above it."

"Something's dug a burrow," Caroline said. "A rabbit or something."

"It's too big for a burrow," Anna said. "It's big enough for a person."

"Maybe a *bear* lives there," Caroline said sarcastically.

"Wouldn't you like to climb all the way down to the river?" Anna said.

"Hmmmmm. Keith's done it lots of times."

"I wouldn't be scared to do it," Anna said. "It'd be fun."

Caroline took in this bit of braggadocio with a faint smile, and then said, "Double-dog-dare-you."

"Coward takes a dare," said Anna, who had always conveniently but honestly understood this answer backwards—that is, if you acted on, took *up* a dare, you were a coward.

Her apparently craven reply seemed to comfort Caroline, who said, "Oh well, I wouldn't do it either. I'd be scared."

Just then they heard a whoop from across the street.

"Tété's calling," Caroline said. "Dinner. We'd better get back over the fence before she sees us."

When Tété took them to task at dinnertime for not coming to tell Margaret goodbye, Caroline said nothing about what had happened, only, "We didn't know she was leaving so early."

"Didn't you hear Cla'ence calling you? Where were you?"

"I don't know," Caroline said, and looked at Tété with a closed blank face, her dreamy eyes cold with the triumph of deceit.

"Hummph!" Tété said.

The next morning Tété got up at five o'clock, as she always did, dressed, unlocked the house, put the water on to boil for her coffee, and went out into the front yard to get the paper. As she told them afterwards, she did not see the paper and realized that one of the dogs must have carried it away. She looked around the yard, and then crossed the street to look in the park. There, as she wandered, she happened to see Caroline's dolls hanging in the tree where the children had forgotten them after their game of Indians the day before.

Muttering gloomily to herself about the fate of children who disobeyed, Tété hitched up her skirts and climbed the fence to retrieve the dolls. She reached out to unfasten one from the branch, and, just as she touched it, the small section of bluff on which she stood caved away under her feet.

Clutching at weeds and roots growing out of the face of the bluff, she slid perhaps ten feet before coming up against the trunk of the small tree in which the dolls were hung. There was a slow tearing of roots and the tree began to heave out of its bed in the loose shale. Tété grabbed with both hands at the bushes above her head and hung on.

Her feet were against the half-uprooted tree, her face against the crumbling dirt of the bluff, her hands clutching a couple of tough privet switches. She had not the strength to pull herself up, and there was no way to go down except by falling. At that hour no one was in sight or even in calling distance, either on the street above her head or on the river bank two hundred feet below her feet. It was quiet all around—no sound except the calls of wakening birds.

"I knew I had to hang on," she said afterwards, "so I said, 'Lord help me,' and I just hung on."

She "hung on" for almost two hours. While the children were still sleeping, the house servants arrived, found her gone, and the pot on the kitchen stove boiled dry and burned black. Clarence, coming out on the front gallery to look up and down Baird Heights Drive, while the maid and the cook conversed in low frightened voices about calling the police or the preacher, found her. For as soon as she heard the front screen door slam, Tété, who had not wasted her voice or her strength calling when no one could hear her, began to shout.

"Cla'ence!" she called. "Cla'ence Jackson? Lucy? Git on over here. I done fell off the bluff." And when she heard him coming at a run, "Look out, now. Stand back. You'll cave off on top of me."

She did not move or raise her head to look up at Clarence, but directed him to go and get some planks and a rope. She had had plenty of time to decide what must be done.

He came back, almost hysterical, his dark face gray. "I can't do it, Miss Tété," he said. "I got Keith up here. He do it."

"You got the planks?" she said.

"Yes'm."

"Keith, lay them boards out, and Cla'ence, you slide out and drop me the rope."

"No'm. Keith, he do it."

"Cla'ence Jackson, you do what I tell you."

"Keith, he's lighter than me. Better he do it."

"Give me the rope, Clarence," Keith said, "and you hold the other end. Tété, be quiet."

He slithered out on the planks, like a man on rotten ice, and dropped a loop of rope down to her while Clarence stood back a safe distance behind the fence, and muttered every now and then to himself, "Lord God, Miss Tété. Jesus save us."

Moving slowly and cautiously, Tété let go one of the privet switches, took hold of the rope and pulled the loop over her head and under her left arm. A shower of dirt rained down on her head and shoulders. She leaned her face against the bluff and did not move for a few minutes. Then she shifted her grip, worked the loop downward over her right arm, and tightened it around her body.

"Now, Keith," she said. "Get back over the fence before y'all start to pull."

Standing on the other side of the fence, Keith and Clarence pulled her up. On the way, Tété grabbed the dolls from the branch where they still hung. When they had pulled her over the crumbling edge of the bluff and helped her across the fence, she gave Clarence one brief, dispassionate look, brushed the dirt and twigs from her clothes, and started home.

"If you had fell off on top of me, Keith," she said, "I'd just as soon have been dead, anyhow."

"There wasn't much chance of that," the boy said.

"I hope y'all got some coffee made," she said. "I ain't had mine yet." She paused and moved her shoulders stiffly, opened and closed her hands several times, touched Keith lightly on the arm, smiled at him, then bent over and began to laugh. "Cla'ence," she said, "you was scared plumb white."

"Come on, Tété," Keith said. "Let's go home."

"Umph," Tété said. She straightened up. And then, "Lord save us, I bet my pot's burnt up, ain't it?"

At home, she inspected the burned pot, made and drank her coffee, bathed and dressed again, and went about her business.

The weekend had gone wrong from the beginning, from the moment Caroline had thought of climbing into the tree and making her mother look for them to say goodbye. And now Anna could not shake off the guilty thought that somehow, perhaps because they had hung the dolls in the tree, perhaps for some obscurer reason, she and Caroline had been responsible for Tété's fall. If such a thought crossed Caroline's mind, she did not say so; but some frightening depth of feeling moved her, this much Anna knew, and silence and secrecy were Caroline's natural response.

Anna did not break the silence by saying aloud what she said to herself: "I want to go *home*." Or, as if she were a baby just learning to talk, simply, "Maa-ma!" Like many children, she was sure that courtesy consisted in concealing one's emotions, and often even one's necessities, if one could, that there was something vaguely disgraceful about open sorrow. And so, when Caroline suggested it, she put on her swimming suit, and Clarence took them to the Elysian Club swimming pool to spend the morning.

It did not seem unusual after lunch when Tété, as she often did on Saturday, shepherded them all into the car, and took them to Selina's.

They drove out into the country mostly silent, although Keith and Caroline exchanged a few words about Keith's horse. Was he still favoring his left foreleg? Had he been shod since he had thrown a shoe on their last ride? Keith, sitting beside Clarence on the front seat, answered Caroline's questions in monosyllables, not turning to look either at Tété or at the two little girls sitting beside her.

After a few minutes, they left the graveled county road and followed a winding dirt wagon track that climbed steadily upward through a stretch of deep woods so thickly grown with Spanish moss that all the trees were dying, past the bare site of what tradition said had once been an Indian village, around the base of a great, round, mysterious mound, toward the high rolling fields and pastures of Selina's farm. In front of Selina's green-roofed white cottage, the track turned on itself in a single loop, and here they drew up.

Selina came out of the house, greeted the children, shook hands with Clarence, and kissed Tété, while Anna looked on curiously. Although she herself kissed Tété at the beginning and end of every summer visit, and recognized the kiss as a token of the deepest significance, it never ceased to astonish her when she saw two colored people kiss each other. It was as if with that gesture they called attention to their own immitigable reality.

The three grown people went into the house, talking.

"Lord, Miss Selina, Miss Tété give us a fright this morning."

"Cla'ence! 'Twasn't nothing."

"Miss Selina, she fell off the bluff. The bluff! Like to scared us out of seven years' growth."

The children scattered—Caroline and Anna carrying stale cornbread to feed the ducks and geese in Selina's pond, and Keith away into the cotton field on the west side of the house where he tramped methodically up one row and down another, as he always did, looking for arrowheads. The afternoon passed like many before and after it, and at dusk the children gathered in the kitchen for supper.

Selina had fried chicken on her big wood-burning kitchen range, and had made biscuits for them. The table by the window was laid with a green-checked oilcloth cover and odds and ends of chipped china in patterns that Anna had seen on the shelves of the Baird pantry. Selina and Clarence were sitting now on the small front porch, talking together in low voices, while Tété served the children and sat down to eat with them.

It was at the supper table that Anna and Caroline found out what the "burrow" they had seen in the face of the bluff really was, although, if they had thought about it, they would probably have guessed when they first saw it.

They knew as soon as they sat down that something was wrong with Keith. He was always quiet, and Anna, although she was sure he liked her, often felt uncomfortable with him. It was as if he were waiting, looking at you expectantly out of his intelligent light green eyes, with a mocking smile, and waiting for some gesture, some word that would make true friendship possible. And yet when you gave it, when you tried, he slipped away, as if after all that were not what he wanted. Tonight he sat in Selina's kitchen, across the table from Tété, with that queer mocking smile on his face, and while he didn't "sass" Tété, everything he said bordered on impudence.

"Your mama be home Monday and tend to you," Tété muttered at last. "You wait."

Keith rose to his feet and with elaborate courtesy handed the biscuits across the table to Anna. "Have a biscuit, Anna," he said. "They're abso*lute*ly delicious."

"I already have two," Anna said. "Thank you."

"Hmmm," he said, and gazed solemnly at her plate. "So you have."

Anna giggled.

"Sit down, Keith," Tété said. "You're tilting the table."

Keith rocked back on his heels and continued to stand.

"Sit down, son," she said. "Finish your supper."

"Can't *you* tend to me, Tété?" he said. "Can't you? You got to wait for Margaret?"

"I could," she said. "Don't you worry about that. I been tending to you for thirteen years and I still could if I wanted to."

"You! You're nothing but . . ." He broke off and sat down. He had shocked himself.

She was shocked, too. "What's the matter with you, Keith Baird?" she said. "Are you out of your mind?"

He shook his head and swayed a little in his chair. "I'm . . . I'm . . ."

Tété got up and came around the table. "Are you sick, son?" she said. She bent over him, looking into his face. "Your eyes are bloodshot," she said, and then, straightening up, stared down at him in incredulous outrage. "Keith Baird, you been in Selina's dewberry wine," she said. "I smell it."

He got up from the table, swaying. "I'm sick," he said. He ran out of the kitchen door into the chicken yard, and vomited. He was trying to get out of sight behind the chicken house, but he could not.

"That's right," she called after him. "You due to be sick. Drinking wine! And I know what's the matter with you, all right. I seen that cave this morning. I wasn't so scared I didn't look around me."

That was the first Anna and Caroline had heard about the cave. They looked at each other in silent surprise, remembering the dark hole they had seen in the face of the bluff.

"Don't you know you fool around that bluff you going to fall smack in the river and never come up?" Tété said.

He retched and coughed, and then he stood in the middle of the yard and yelled back at her. "It's mine," he shouted. "You hear me? It's mine, and you keep away from it."

"You reckon I would've been down there if I could've helped it?" she said. "And anyhow 'tain't much of yours now. It's half full of dirt from that slide." She did not say that the slide had been caused by his digging in the bluff, and perhaps, after all, it wasn't.

"I know it's full of dirt," Keith said, "but I can fix it." He walked over to the cistern by the back door, pumped some water over his head, washed his mouth out, and got a drink.

Tété had followed him into the yard, and now she stood by the cistern watching him. "You stay off the bluff, Keith," she said. "I'm telling you, you stay off it, or you'll be sorry."

Keith stood up, shook the water out of his hair, and stared at her for a moment, his green eyes full of hatred. Then he turned and ran away toward the horse lot.

"Don't you go off," Tété called after him. "We got to go back to town in a little bit. It's 'most dark."

But he caught his horse, bridled it, and rode down the turn row, bareback, at a gallop, Tété looking after him anxiously. "What he want with a cave, anyhow?" she said to Caroline. "A great big grown boy like him!" And then, "Wine! Drinking *wine!*"

Caroline did not reply.

A little later he came riding back, slow and sheepish. After all, there was no place for him to go. He watered his horse at the pond, put him up, and wandered into the house, looking as if he wished he could apologize.

"It's all right, son," Tété said. She was scouring a skillet at Selina's sink, while Selina, standing at the drainboard beside her, was

drying dishes. "You rid it out," she said, "and I been scrubbing it out. Now, let's go home."

No more was said that night about the cave or about the wine, and, as far as Anna knew, Tété did not mention either to Margaret when she returned from New Orleans. At any rate, no punishment followed for Keith. Nor did Tété tell Margaret the real reason she had climbed over the fence that morning.

"Sweet," she said when Margaret asked her, "I done already told you. I thought I seen something in a tree."

"Something in a tree! What, for goodness' sake?"

"'Twasn't nothing," Tété said. "I just *thought* I seen it."

III

DURING THE WINTER, at home in Eureka, the little west-central Louisiana town where Ralph and Charlotte McGovern and their family lived, Anna heard talk of "financial difficulties." The Homochitto Bank and Trust Company failed. Old Mrs. McGovern's comfortable income from her husband's estate was wiped out, and Ralph undertook her support. The Bairds, so Anna heard, were "ruined" by the failure of the bank and the loss of income from downtown rental property which stood empty following the failure of one business after another. Keith Baird, Sr., secure in his youth and wealth, had not had much life insurance when he died, and what he had left, Margaret, equally secure and heedless, had long since spent. In short, suddenly, catastrophically, incredibly, there was no money. No money even to pay the grocery bill or the servants' salaries; no money to pay the taxes on the house.

Other women in Margaret's predicament—educated for marriage and leisure—would consider themselves lucky if they were allowed to stay on in houses that could not be sold for taxes. They would go to work in the WPA sewing rooms for eleven dollars a week, plant a patch of greens in the backyard, and from time to time sell a piece of family furniture or silver to some more affluent cousin who "couldn't bear to let it go out of the family." But not Margaret. She assessed her situation with a cold intelligent eye and went to work.

"Would anyone have dreamed it was possible!" Charlotte said to Ralph at the dinner table, the day she learned in a letter from one of her sisters that Margaret was opening a tearoom. "Margaret Baird of all people! I always thought she was helpless as a child." And then to her son, "Put your napkin in your lap, Ralph, and sit up straight."

"Margaret?" Ralph stood at the other end of the table with the carving knife and fork in his hands, thoughtfully examining the roast. "Don't worry about Margaret," he said. "She'll stay on top of the game." He began to carve, slowly and methodically, his big blunt hands manipulating the tools with careful skill.

"Why, Ralph!" Charlotte said.

"What do you mean, 'stay on top of the game?'" Anna said to her father.

He continued to carve without answering, and Anna looked at her mother, who was sitting at the opposite end of the table with the letter still in her hand. "Helpless as a child?" "On top of the game?" What did these words have to do with Margaret—the gay and lovely, carefree Margaret whose glamour and poise were enough to fill the heart of an awkward eleven-year-old girl with despair. Were grown people, after all, sometimes helpless, sometimes not on top of every game? She looked from her mother to her father again. Certainly not them, not her mother, whose round pretty face and determined chin said quite plainly that she would know what to do in any emergency; or her father—what earthquake could budge him, could make him carve the roast with the grain?

"What do you mean?" she said again.

"Hmm," Ralph said. "Charlotte, this knife needs sharpening," and he went to the kitchen for the whetstone.

Charlotte looked up from her letter. "Father means that Margaret has plenty of sense," she said, "that he thinks, if she has to, she'll be a good manager."

And indeed she was.

She induced the widower from Baton Rouge to put up the necessary capital, paid off the taxes on her house, bought the minimum of equipment from a bankrupt "confectionary," and opened her little tearoom in one of the downstairs rooms of the garçonnière. With Tété's help, she began a modest catering service for weddings and parties. The rest of the garçonnière, seven rooms, was let out to "single gentlemen with references," and the house itself was opened to tourists traveling between Memphis and New Orleans. A sign lettered in Old English script hung by the front gate:

See The Shadows—built 1816

Admission—$1.00

Tearoom

Lunch 12–2   Dinner 6–10

Catering

Margaret thrived in her new role. It suited her personality and character quite well to be on stage, as it were, as the struggling chatelaine of an aristocratic house fallen on hard times. Everyone was astonished to see her master, without apparent difficulty, the complexities of a restaurant and catering service, while at the same time she saw that her house was spotless for the inspection of tourists, and ran what amounted to a small hotel, all without seeming to be ruffled, hurried, perplexed, or even "busy."

To the most acute observer it appeared that Margaret's party—the long celebration, the gathering of *bon vivants* that her adult life had been—continued to go on. The roomers, the tourists, the customers in the tearoom—all were guests. One was tempted not to pay the bill, out of delicacy, for fear that an exchange of money would offend the hostess.

If it was true, as Charlotte was to observe the following summer, that Margaret now had even less time for her children than she had had in the old days, it was also true that she contrived to make a life for them and for her household under circumstances that were driving people all about her into apathy, alcoholism, despair, and suicide. Not only did she not fire any of her servants, she managed to hire more. The maids became part-time waitresses; Clarence was put into a white jacket and turned into a headwaiter; and there were two more cooks in the kitchen. If Selina's house in the country needed a coat of paint or a patched roof, Margaret had the work done, and Selina paid it out in vegetables and milk for the tearoom.

Besides, the children were growing up now and a mother's constant loving attention was no longer necessary to them. They did not want it. In a year or so, by Margaret's standards, Keith should be sent away to school; and the day was imminent when Caroline would need evening dresses, parties, and, eventually, college or a good finishing school. These were necessities, and the money must be found to make them possible.

Everything was different. There were no more leisurely four o'clock dinners for half the town; instead, the kitchen was an assembly line for the making of everything from dozens of cucumber sandwiches to big pots of steaming gumbo. By the summer of 1932 the household was entirely reorganized, even to the places where everyone slept. In 1931 Keith and Caroline and Tété had still lived in the nursery apartment in the garçonnière—a huge playroom downstairs (the tearoom now), and upstairs a bedroom for each of them, and two baths. Now the whole family lived in the big house. The two children and Margaret had the three upstairs bedrooms and Tété lived downstairs, where Margaret had converted the study off the dining room and next to the downstairs bath into a room for her. She was sixty-five years old and was beginning to suffer from the rheumatism that, as the years passed, would be increasingly crippling and painful. The stairs were hard for her to climb, and she went up only two or three times a week to make sure that the maid was keeping things properly spotless.

Tété's big room on the south side of the house, sunny in winter and shaded in the late spring and summer by a huge chestnut oak tree, was furnished like the rest of the house with Baird family furniture— a double tester bed with spool posts, a Victorian love seat and parlor chairs, and a heavy walnut armoire. In no sense of the word could the room have been described as "servant's quarters."

Here Tété lived, or, as it sometimes seemed to Anna, held court. Here she sat in the morning sunshine with a basket of mending at her feet, occasionally giving directions to one or another of the servants; here she received her callers—Selina and Selina's grown children, her brother Aaron, Clara Winston who was Homochitto's fine laundress and Tété's closest friend, and Clara's sister, the town's "French" seamstress, who had served her apprenticeship in a New Orleans dressmaker's shop. If the children went into the room, they too went as callers. She received them as she would have in her own house.

During those years Anna continued to spend a part of every summer vacation with the Bairds. She saw but paid almost no attention

to the changes in the household. When tourists came through the house and stopped to stare and comment on the fine Hepplewhite secretary in the south parlor, the collection of Waterford glass in the dining room, or on the children themselves, she was delighted.

I *belong* here, she would think to herself with a surge of self-important joy. Look at me, I belong here. It may be that she felt she was in her way as curious and interesting a sight as the Hepplewhite secretary. Why, she did not inquire, but then she did not really wonder why they wanted to look at the secretary.

She scarcely noticed, either, that Caroline's toys grew shabbier and that no new toys were bought, that the children's horses had been sold, that the blue Buick, apparently beyond repair, was up on blocks in the carriage house, and the black Cadillac was turning purple with age.

She did observe, however, or rather, it was forced on her attention, that Tété hated the tourists.

It happened one morning when the children were going out of the house as a group of touring ladies was coming in. Keith, fifteen now, and, except for an occasional hunting companion, solitary as he had always been, had been coaxed out of his absorption in a book and persuaded to drive the two girls to the swimming pool. As they came down the stairs, Tété was opening the front door. The ladies came in, nodding feathered hats at one another and chattering like parrots in rolling midwestern voices, while Tété, in her full-skirted dark dress and white apron, her hair screwed into half a dozen small knots bound close to her scalp with rubber bands, her lower lip characteristically thrust out (this alone was no sign of ill humor), stood patiently by, waiting for them to be silent so that she could take their money and guide them through the house.

As the children approached, one of the ladies was saying to another, "Eleanor-r-r-r! Will you look! Isn't she a *picture?*" And then to Tété, "I'll bet you're these children's old nurse, aren't you? And you've been with the family for just years and *year-r-rs.*"

For a long moment Tété did not answer. Then, "Yes'm," she said, her face expressionless.

"And do they call you 'Mammy?'" another of the women asked. "I'll just bet you call her Mammy, don't you, children?"

The three children stood staring at the women. Anna was stricken with a paralyzing embarrassment, and it crossed her mind in a flash of horror that Tété might drop dead of rage on the spot. She looked down at the floor and said nothing.

Keith stepped between Tété and the women. He had grown quite tall in the past year, and, standing in front of Tété, hid her almost completely from the strangers.

"No," he said. "We don't call her Mammy. She . . ." He stopped, as if he could not bear to speak of Tété to these people, either by her name or as "she." "We employ . . ." he said, and then, ". . . house-keeper."

Tété peered out from behind him. "If you ladies will step into the south parlor," she said, "I'll show you . . ."

Anna fled.

Caroline followed more slowly, and then Keith, closing the front door carefully behind him.

Perhaps it was this incident that made Anna begin to notice how the Bairds made Tété's life pleasant in a dozen subtle ways, how, if they were together on the street either Keith or Caroline always dropped back to walk with her and to help her up and down the curbs, how they protected her from the inevitable guest who talked of the peculiarities of Negroes as if all the servants were deaf, how Margaret read aloud to her in the evening, and planned the family celebration for her birthday. She saw that the checkers games that she and Caroline still played with Tété were turned quite around. Now, instead of Tété's sometimes losing to one of them on purpose, they had to lose to her. They no longer had any interest in checkers, if the truth be known, but Tété as she got older developed an increasing passion for the game. She moved her lips in deep concentration as she bent over the board, pushing her men about and hastily retrieving them, plotting ways to outwit her opponents. Here, at least, her devotion to reality was in abeyance; by the time they were thirteen, Anna and Caroline knew that they had to let her win at least two-thirds of the time.

It was during those years, too, that Anna began to think with detachment of and to marvel at Tété's life. How had it happened in the distant past, long before even Margaret was born, that she had come into her role? Had there been some final decision taken when she had said to herself, like Ruth to Naomi, "Thy people shall be my people?" Had she renounced a lover, actively refused a life among her own kind and kindred? And if she had, why? For security? Prestige? Love? Had it been, perhaps, because from the beginning she had seen in the Bairds a way to make her family secure? They *were* secure, Selina and her children and her children's children, as Negroes seldom were in Homochitto. Their houses were painted, their farm was their own, the grandchildren were going to college, and one could not explain it except through Tété.

Or had the role, the life she led, come on Tété so slowly out of childhood and early youth, that she herself did not know what had happened, how it had come about that she lived in isolated splendor among white people, and in her Victorian bedroom with its ornately carved sofa, its crisp chintz drapes and Marseilles bedspread, received the Negro friends and relatives who had left behind them the warm sweaty disorder of shotgun houses, shooed the chickens out of the way, latched their scrappy wooden gates, and come to call?

By the fall of 1934 Margaret was able to send Keith away to school. His education had been the first goal toward which she had begun to work, as soon as she had seen that she could make a success of the tearoom, and for a year she had talked of it insistently to him and to her friends: He must go to the preparatory school where his father had gone, and then to Harvard. A man must get a decent education, and this was not possible in Mississippi, perhaps not even in the South. Besides, he should spend some time in the East, visit his father's people, and find out what the world was like. And there were contacts to be made. It was out of the question for him to think of settling in Homochitto. What did Homochitto have to offer him, now that the Baird money was gone? Could anyone imagine him running a tearoom!

To Keith, this was the burden of what she said. But to her friends she said a great many other things, things overheard from time to time by Anna and Caroline, and sometimes even by Keith, although Margaret did not intend him to overhear. But he stayed a great deal at home, and Margaret's voice was penetrating.

"He needs to get out of this household of women and have some contact with men," she said to Charlotte one day. "I'm at my wit's end with him."

She and Charlotte were sitting on the screened upstairs gallery of the Baird house that June morning, "visiting," a luxury Margaret could not often indulge herself in now that she was a business-woman. Margaret, in a heavy white, crepe de chine negligee left from wealthier days, and badly scuffed white satin mules, lay on the chaise longue and smoked, while Charlotte, her dark hair neatly waved, her fresh cotton housedress crisp with starch, sat with a straw work basket beside her and rolled up a ball of rag strips for the crocheted rug she was making.

From the bedroom at the back of the house came the faint sound of guitar music, and a boy's voice shouting gaily above the chords, "M' yalla, oh, m' yalla, oh, m' yalla gal. M' yalla, oh, m' yalla, oh, m' yalla gal."

"He's so *big*," Margaret said. "It's ridiculous for Tété and me to be in charge of that great big *man*." She sighed.

Charlotte creased and rolled the strips of cloth from the pile in her basket, and nodded sympathetically.

"I just don't know where Keith comes from," Margaret said. "He's certainly not like his father. Keith was so *gregarious*. And while he has my coloring, he's not like me either." She laughed. "I used to tell him he was our changeling," she said. "Our gypsy child. Just listen to him now." She gestured toward the back of the house. "He'll sit back there for *hours*, playing that guitar. He's absolutely obsessed with it. And now—Lord knows where Keith heard about him—he's made friends with a colored man who used to play in some jazz band down in New Orleans—Jesse, his name is. Keith goes out to his house and sits on the porch with him by the hour, playing the guitar, while Jesse plays the Jew's harp or the fiddle, or sings. Apparently he (the colored man, I mean) can play anything. That's where Keith picks up all these queer songs.

"Oh, I suppose there's no harm in it. It's not that. And the re-markable thing is, the colored people love it. Tété says they all think Keith is very good on the guitar. By the time the two of them have been playing an hour or so, they'll have the whole neighborhood gathered round listening. Still, there's no use denying it, it may be all right, but it makes me *nervous*. And Tété doesn't approve at *all*. She thinks it would be better if Jesse came here—but Keith won't have it that way.

"And if he's not with Jesse," she went on, "he's in the woods all day or on the river, *by himself*. It's not natural. He doesn't seem to care if he ever sees another boy. And not only that. When do you suppose he is going to grow up? Do you know he has never had an engagement with a girl—*a date*—in his life? That in itself is enough to drive you crazy. Is he going to be one of these men who don't like women? Mercy, at his age, I'll bet his *father* . . ." She broke off.

"Give him time, Margaret," Charlotte said. "He's only sixteen, after all. And he's shy. He'll come along at his own speed." She dropped the ball of rags into her lap and gazed out across the river. "Sometimes I think Keith has a streak of McGovern," she said. "You know how solitary the McGovern men are, and how they love the woods. And they're inclined to be studious, too." She picked up her work and went on firmly. "You ought to be glad Keith is such a good student and gets so much pleasure out of his music," she said. "If his grades weren't so splendid, he would never have gotten a scholarship."

But Margaret paid no attention. "I used to think how grand it would be to take him to New York, to travel with him, when he got to be a young man," she said. "Do you remember what a beautiful baby he was? I thought to myself, how lovely to go to the theater with him as an escort, to see him in his first dinner jacket, so tall and handsome, to introduce him everywhere as *my* son. Although, really," she added, "I know I shouldn't say this but it's true—he's not so much handsome, he's more, *beautiful*. Too bad Caroline didn't get his looks. Anyhow, you know what I mean; I'd be so *proud* of him. It would be . . . lovely . . ." She shrugged. "But he's not interested," she said, "even if we still had the money."

In his bedroom Keith struck a series of drumlike bass notes on the guitar: "Standing at the crossroads, I try to flag a ride. Ain't nobody seem to know me, everybody pass me by," he sang.

Margaret made an irritated face. "That's that awful, *gloomy* 'Crossroads Blues,'" she said. "I reckon Jesse taught it to him. He sings it *constantly*."

"Most boys Keith's age aren't interested in escorting their mothers anywhere," Charlotte said, "except maybe into some dark closet where they would never have to be seen again."

"But I don't want him to be just another *adolescent*," Margaret said. "We don't live like that. And I always felt that . . . that a certain amount of formality kept children from hating their parents so *intimately*. Like the English, and nannies, and tutors and so on. Tété's been a buffer like that, so that to Keith and Caroline I should be more of a *friend*. Mama always said the same thing, you know. And she was right.

"Besides, I deserve a little companionship in my old age." (This was one of Margaret's games. She had begun to touch up the gray streaks in her lovely, curly, dark hair, and she looked younger than her thirty-nine years, but she was forever referring to Caroline as the child of her old age, or speaking of herself as if she were on the brink of senility.) "I do," she said. "You needn't laugh. It's time for Keith to realize that he's going to have to take his father's place one of these days."

Charlotte took these remarks in silence, but after some minutes she said, "You're just talking to hear yourself talk, Margaret. You know Keith can't take his father's place. Of course, he has to assume his responsibilities, but in his own way, after all."

"Well, that's what I mean," Margaret said. "I'm just going to get tired one of these days, and that's the truth. I'm a woman who needs someone to *lean* on."

Charlotte laughed. "My dear," she said, "you need someone to lean on about like you need a third leg. What you mean is you want everybody to behave themselves."

"Well, it would help," Margaret said. "It would make life a lot simpler." Without warning or apparent cause, for she had been speaking lightly, with the ironic smile and exaggerated emphasis of one who regards his problems dispassionately, and considers them slightly ridiculous, Margaret's green eyes filled with tears. She looked down at her lap and drew a deep breath, obviously trying to recover herself. Charlotte said nothing.

Then Margaret looked up. "Everything is so different from what I ever thought it would be," she said.

Then, "There are some people who are just meant to be rich. I always knew that, and of course that's one reason I married Keith." She began to cry in earnest.

Charlotte got up and went over to her and patted her gently on the shoulder. "I know what a struggle you're having, my dear," she said.

Margaret got a handkerchief out of her pocket and wiped her eyes. "We were so *safe*," she said. "Do you remember that, Charlotte? When we were children? Nothing ever changed then."

"I don't suppose there's any way left in the world to be safe," Charlotte said, "except . . ."

"I don't know *why* I feel so anxious these days," Margaret said. "It's not just money. I was lying about that. But everything is so difficult. The children . . . Where did I get those two queer quiet children, Charlotte? They ought to be yours and Ralph's instead of Keith's and mine. Oh, I know you're right; we have that same quiet streak in the family that the McGoverns have. Poor Aunt Anne never said two consecutive sentences in her life that I can remember. But, after all, that's two generations back. And Tété . . . Keith has gotten so sullen lately, sometimes I think he *hates* Tété. Why? What's the matter with us all?"

Charlotte opened her mouth to speak, but Margaret shook her head. "No," she said. "Don't tell me. After all, even if anyone could, I might not want to know."

"Love . . ." Charlotte said, and broke off.

"I know. You McGoverns think love, loyalty, and impeccable morals are the answers to everything. You've always been better at suffering and less inclined to enjoy sinning than the Bairds. But I don't *want* to suffer. No, not at all. I want to have a good time, and I want the children to behave themselves and have a good time, too. It's so simple, if you just know how, and, as you said, if everybody behaves."

"Behaves? Who's not behaving?" The sound of music from Keith's room had broken off several minutes earlier, although neither Charlotte nor Margaret had noticed it, and now they looked up and saw the boy standing in the doorway, his guitar still in his hands, the dark beauty of his rosy face and sea green eyes made somehow intolerably heartbreaking by the awkward angles of his thin arms and legs and the bruised knobs of his knees below his shorts. His voice was changing, and, as he spoke, broke on the second syllable of "behaving," and went up at least a fifth. He made a face of boredom and self-contempt. "Margaret," he said, in a voice so low they could scarcely hear him, "if you don't mind my calling it to your attention, the *children* are in Caroline's room and can hear every word you're saying."

Margaret's face flooded with color. Then, "They're not paying any attention to us, Keith," she said. "And besides, I haven't said a single word I would be ashamed for any of you to hear."

"Haven't you?" he said.

Charlotte, unwilling to be present at a family quarrel, gathered her scraps of cloth and thread into her basket and stood up; but Keith turned away without saying any more, and in a moment they heard him going down the stairs.

"No," Margaret said. "Don't go, Charlotte. He's all right." And

when they had heard the front door close behind him, "I didn't, did I? I didn't say anything wrong."

From the gallery, they saw him going down the front walk and across the street to the park. He stood at the edge of the bluff for a long time, leaning on the fence and gazing out across the slow-moving breadth of the brown river toward the western horizon, where a little oxbow lake gleamed like a new sickle in the morning sun. Then he left the park, and, after pausing for a moment to glance up at them, started off northward at a brisk walk, his guitar slung by a leather strap from his shoulder.

"He's going to see his *friend* again, I suppose," Margaret said. "Jesse, I mean. You see what I'm talking about? I don't know what to do with him. Tété says I shouldn't let him speak to me like that, and certainly she never let me speak to Mama like that; but she's getting old, you know, and she can't control Keith, that's the plain truth. And you know I've never been a disciplinarian—never wanted to be. I can't change my character overnight." Again her eyes filled with tears, and she brushed them impatiently away.

"You have to overlook some things in a boy that age," Charlotte said. "He's got to learn to be independent."

"Can't he find any way to do that except by hating us all? Mercy! I'll be glad when he gets married and I can turn him over to some other woman. He's nothing but a nuisance."

"Don't worry so much about him, Margaret," Charlotte said. "You're doing the right thing. A boys' school is probably just what he needs. And hold in your mind what a fine boy he is—so handsome and intelligent and *gentle*. He is, you know. And he'll get bravely over hating you in a year or two, and be a good man—the comfort and support of your old age."

Margaret laughed. "I reckon all we can do is keep our fingers crossed," she said.

Afterwards Charlotte told Ralph that she was worried about Keith. "He's such a lonely boy," she said. "My heart goes out to him. But what could I say? There's no way for them to be anything but what they are." She did not really believe herself when she said this, but, confronted with their distress, she said what was charitable. Unable to leave it at that, however, she added, "But Tété . . ." And then, after a thoughtful pause, "You know, Ralph, I can remember hearing Mama talk about Tété when she first came to the Bairds—years ago, before we were born. She was a child—no more than ten or eleven. Her mother died in the street in front of the Bairds' house; it was in one of the last big yellow-fever epidemics. Someone came out of the house, and there she was, dead, with the children sitting on the curb by her body. They weren't Homochitto Negroes; no one knew where they came from. I don't think Tété knew, herself. The Bairds (Margaret's grandmother, I mean) gave the younger children, Selina and Aaron, to Clara Winston's family to raise, and took Tété in to help out in the kitchen." She broke off and sighed. "Mama told me she was nothing but a scarecrow then, a bag of bones and terror. For months she scarcely spoke a word. While now . . ."

"You have to remember that Tété is only a servant," Ralph said. "You mustn't let your imagination run away with you."

But Charlotte shook her head. "I don't know what Tété is," she said. "But I know, whatever it is, it doesn't always work."

IV

AS IT TURNED OUT, school was not successful for Keith. He had no trouble with his studies, for he was bright, but he ran away twice during the first semester. In neither case did he try to come home. He hitchhiked (unmarked by anyone, for in those days of 1934 and 1935 there were plenty of young boys on the road, wandering from town to town, picking up work where they could, sleeping in the open, or finding a night's shelter in one of the hobo camps that were scattered over the country) and worked his way to a nearby city. Both times, however, he had second thoughts, and after a few days telephoned his mother to put an end to her frantic search for him. He was not contrite, but almost against his will, as it seemed, forced himself to tell her where he was, because he had not the ruthlessness of character to continue to make her suffer.

"I was getting along O.K.," he said the second time. "It would have been a lot better if I could have stayed."

That was all he would say. What went unmentioned and un-accounted for were his confusion and misery—a misery so intense that, in that desperate time when it was not impossible he might have starved or died of exposure on the road, he had risked the brutality and insecurity of an alien world, not once but twice.

After the second incident the headmaster at his school wrote Margaret that any further escapades would mean expulsion.

He came home for the Christmas holidays, his reserve, if possible, more impenetrable than ever. No amount of attention from either Margaret or Tété touched him; and in fact he seemed to find the least gesture of love unbearable. It was as if he knew some shocking secret and was afraid that, if anyone breached his privacy, he might forget himself and tell it. One saw on his face an expression familiar to every mother of a young boy, of affected boredom, that is of boredom covering another emotion which one felt was probably revulsion.

It is almost always true that one cannot, perhaps even should not, reach a child in this sort of crisis. He must resolve it for himself. But meanwhile, everyone who cares for him recognizes how dire, how far-reaching the consequences may be, and looks back in wonder at the years of his childhood, saying to himself, "Where did it all begin? What happened?"

Several years later, when she was nearly grown, thinking of the events of that winter and the following summer, Anna was to say to herself and to her mother that Margaret must have known Keith was headed for some kind of trouble, that it was unforgivable of her not to have done something to help him, that it was obvious a boarding school was the worst possible place for him. Surely she saw (she had plenty of sense, after all) that Keith had more to take into account than most boys his age—not one mother, but two, each peculiarly unfitted for any category he might try to put her in; not a living, loving father, but a dead one, embalmed forever in his successful gregarious youth; not a family united in comfortable likeness and stability, but one split, yes—she repeated herself—*split*, in time between feckless wealth and hardworking poverty, and in status between black and white.

But Charlotte was to shake her head. How could anyone be sure what had been right and what wrong? What error and what accident? It was all too complicated, and the roots went too far back, to times before Keith, perhaps even before Margaret was born.

"Now what exactly do you mean by that?" Anna said. "Are you going to blame it on original sin?"

But Charlotte would not answer except to say, "We're all supposed to be Christians, and that's the Christian explanation."

"For everything that happens? You mean you think there's nothing we can do about anything?"

"Anna!" Charlotte said. And then, "You're too old to start an argument with me about religion."

At the time it had been going on, however, no one had had even that much explanation. They had all been, in varying degrees, depending upon their involvement, simply worried.

Margaret's reaction to her worry, to the continuous attrition of an insoluble problem, was to put her attention on Caroline. The tearoom now was practically running itself and, as she told everyone, she needed something to occupy her mind.

The widower from Baton Rouge had died quite suddenly that fall, dropped dead of a heart attack, intestate, and although she had been fond of him, even to all appearances in love with him at various times during the past ten years, she was unable to let herself suffer the pain of his death. She never mentioned him except once, when she had had a couple of drinks too many, to Charlotte. "He should have left a will," she said. "It was inexcusable." And, "All those years of friendship and I haven't even a keepsake. The least his children could have done would have been to send me something to remember him by. Anything—a ring, or a tieclasp, or an old pair of shoes. I wouldn't care what it was."

So she turned to Caroline. She would begin to "bring her out a bit," since Keith would not "behave," and since she no longer had anyone to "play with." Or so it seemed to a great many people who had never approved of Margaret in the first place.

Although Charlotte, and later Anna, would detect an unmistakable disappointment in Margaret that Caroline was not a beauty and had neither the personality nor the inclination to be a real "belle," it was also obvious to them, at least to Charlotte, that Margaret intended to make the most of what she considered her daughter's assets.

As for Anna, she was never sure how much she had seen at the time and how much she had learned from her mother, or remembered in later years in an entirely different way from what seemed to be happening when she was present. She knew immediately, however, when she arrived in Homochitto for her summer visit in 1935, that Caroline was as different from her friend of a year ago as if she were another person.

Caroline, already grown to her full height of five feet seven inches, was big-boned and broad-shouldered, and there was almost nothing Margaret could do to conceal the childish thinness of her long arms and legs; but careful attention to clothes and makeup fostered an illusion of maturity. The straight brown hair had been allowed to grow to shoulder length, thick and shining, the ends just turned up with a trace of permanent wave. Braces, worn only at night, had pushed the teeth into an even white line. There was no getting around her nose; it was too big. (Anna overheard this remark.) But her wide, straight mouth had its own shy charm, and her eyes, blue as the sea under the broken arcs of dark brows, had in them sometimes an expression of gentle tenderness that was full of promise for her maturity.

It was not only in appearance that Anna found Caroline different. The truth was that, with her mother's fostering, she had become a young lady. Neither imaginary adventures, backwards letters, days in the country, nor checkers games interested her any longer, but only *boys*. Even a morning's swim was different now. Caroline brushed her brown hair until it shone, and lay on the bank of the pool with suntan oil on her back. The boys in her class at school played water polo or tag, or, sitting on each other's shoulders, fought uproarious battles in the pool, and she watched them with wide-eyed admiration. When one sat down beside her on the bank for a few minutes, she smiled her shy, loving smile, and talked to him in low conspiratorial tones. Anna was bored to distraction.

By the standards of her own class and time, Margaret, to do her justice, did not really "push" Caroline. In the South girls are expected to mature younger than they do in the North, and in small towns, where there are no debuts, and where it is possible to be fairly sure where your children are at all times, simply because there are not many places to go and you know everyone they might meet, it is not unusual for a girl of fourteen to be a young lady, to have "dates," and to go to dances and parties that include all ages.

Nor did Caroline resist being "brought out." She acquiesced absent-mindedly in whatever was done to her or required of her, and seemed content with her mother's attention, whatever its terms. The fits of wild, "queer" defiance of her childhood had vanished, and in their place was a malleable expectancy, as if she were suddenly aware of all the world's inviting possibilities.

But none of this interested Anna. She was thinking only of herself. Physically she was a child, and what it was about boys that made them so fascinating escaped her. All she understood was that Caroline was different. She felt uncomfortable with her old friend, always heretofore so ready for adventure, and shed private tears, not only at being deserted, but at the nebulous conviction that there was something immoral about growing up. Perhaps it was the same impulse of fear and revulsion that rejects foreigners as both immoral and threatening: the instinctive knowledge that whatever is different can be taken into account only at the cost of sacrificing some part of one's own laboriously constructed universe—a sacrifice that, one feels, may very well lead to the collapse of the whole structure. For surely there is nothing more threatening and foreign to the world of sheltered childhood and unawakened virginity than the demands, the urgencies, and responsibilities of sexual maturity.

All these unadmitted, necessarily unrecognizable pressures must be bound into what one thinks of a young girl's "prissy" refusal to take part at fourteen in a game of post office, although, at fifteen, feeling for the first time the exigencies of desire, she may seriously be contemplating elopement.

At any rate, it was true that Anna did not then understand very much about what had happened to make her and Caroline strangers, and she spent an unhappy week finding it out. For she had accepted without thought the Bairds' customary invitation for a summer visit; and, as the days passed, she knew it had been a mistake. She could think of no polite way to go home. Caroline was gentle and courteous. She tried, with a sophistication and consideration that made Anna even more uncomfortable, to draw Anna into her new life; but Anna did not know how to respond. And she was sure in her own mind, although Caroline gave her no reason for her conviction, that Caroline was as anxious to get rid of her as she was to go. She was unspeakably miserable. It did not cross her mind that this visit would shortly be over and that another summer things might be different. Like homesickness, her pain was as real as a toothache or an acute attack of appendicitis. Scarcely able to eat, she concealed her misery and went through the motions that courtesy required, unable to imagine that she would ever be happy again.

To complicate that summer visit, there was another guest in the house. Keith, when he came home from school, brought a friend.

During the second semester he had suddenly become involved in a passionate intimacy with a boy in his class. John Kimbrough—The Count, as Keith and other admiring friends called him—was a big, strongly built boy with a shock of curly blond hair and handsome features that were a trifle too small and squeezed too close together in the middle of his face. He was the son of a Mississippi Delta planter whose views on the world, as reflected in the boy, became only too apparent as his visit progressed: a condescension toward women that took the form of a continuous sniping at the girls and an exaggerated courtliness toward Margaret ("He makes me feel as if I'm either feeble-minded or dying," she told Caroline and Anna), and a virulent contempt for "niggers" that showed itself in his private conversation and kept all the family on the *qui vive* to cover a failure of courtesy toward Tété or one of the maids.

"What on earth does Keith see in him?" Margaret said to anyone who would listen. "He's *impossible*."

"Well, he likes the woods and all," Caroline said. "The river. And hunting and fishing. I don't think he's all that bad—and he's awfully good-looking."

Anna, who took Margaret's mild disapproval more seriously than it was probably meant, and was unreasonably inclined to blame

The Count for her own misery, thought he was worse than "all that bad," and ugly as sin besides, with all his features squinched together in the middle of his face. She said nothing.

"Mostly Keith likes it that he's different from us," Tété said. "You know, Sweet, a boy got to try out new ways before he can settle into old."

All of a sudden, toward the end of the first week of his visit, The Count fell in love with Caroline. No one knew what to make of it. One day he was slyly sticking out his foot to trip her, or asking her in a loud voice at the swimming pool which of the boys she "liked"; the next he was following her about the house with a hangdog expression, as if he hoped she would drop something just so he could pick it up. Caroline was delighted. He might be, in comparison with Keith, a bit slow, lacking in the subtlety, the complexity of personality to which she was used, but he was handsome, and above all he was seventeen—a man of the world.

As for Keith, it had probably not occurred to him that his sister was no longer a child. Anna caught him staring first at Caroline and then at her, as if he had never seen them before and did not know what to make of either of them.

"Do you remember the time my horse stepped on your foot and wouldn't get off?" he said to Anna one morning at the pool, as if proving to himself that at least they had been children.

The Count and Caroline were lying side by side on a beach towel a few yards away, their faces turned toward each other. They had been talking seriously together for half an hour, paying no attention to anyone else.

"Out at Selina's?" Anna said. "Uh-huh. But you got him to move. Remember?"

Keith laughed. "You hollered so loud the horse was paralyzed with fright," he said.

"Well, after all, it did break my toe," Anna said. "It hurt."

She pointed to a small child standing at the edge of the pool with his head bent almost to his knees, both hands pointing at the water. "Do you remember what a hard time you had teaching us to dive?" she said. "We'd stand like that for ages, trying to get up the nerve to go in head first."

Keith nodded and they smiled at each other tentatively, each one seeking an ally in the curious situation in which they found themselves.

And in fact they were trapped with each other. If The Count wanted to take Caroline to the movies or for a drive, Anna, of course, had to go along, since she was Caroline's guest, and Keith had to escort her or stay at home. Once, at the movies, tentatively experimenting with the notion of courting, Keith held Anna's hand until it was clammy with sweat. She felt as if her brain had moved out of her head and lodged itself at the end of her arm, and she could not keep her attention on the movie for more than a moment or two at a time.

Afterwards, walking home, he began to talk openly and naturally about their situation. "You know, we're pretty much like a sister and brother," he said. "You've been around an awful lot for an awful long time."

In an unaccountable access of courage and frankness, Anna said, "I didn't want you to hold my hand. It was your idea." And having been so bold and honest, she was suddenly filled with joy, as if a strong wind had blown away the misery that had oppressed her for days. She gave a little skip and laughed aloud.

He looked at her with a familiar, comforting expression of self-derision on his face. "It was a pretty silly idea, wasn't it?"

"Yes. *We* don't have to be any different from always," she said.

"I didn't mean that, exactly. I'm different all right. The Count has taught me a lot I didn't know."

"The Count!" Anna said, still intoxicated with her own courage. "I'll bet."

"He's a terrific guy, really he is," Keith said. "He knows how to manage—to stay on top of the game."

Anna thought of what her father had said about Margaret, the same words; but surely he had not meant the same thing. "Hmmm," she said.

"He's the best basketball player I've ever seen, and he's been to Europe, and . . ." Keith broke off, as if unwilling to confide other far more interesting things that The Count had done. "He's widely experienced for his age," he said.

"There are some things you don't need to go to Europe to know," Anna said.

"Like what?"

"Like why does he stick out his foot and trip you just for meanness, and why does he say the things he says when he knows Clarence and Tété and everybody can hear him?"

"He's just kidding you," Keith said. "And as for the other, things are different in the Delta from the way they are down here."

Anna had not the least idea what he meant by that, but, anxious to please him, she nodded wisely, and said, "Oh."

Abruptly Keith changed the subject. "Did you know I have a girl?" he said.

"You have!" Anna was astonished. "Why don't you ever have a date with her?"

"Not here. At school—I mean she lives up there. But don't say anything about it. If there's anything I hate, it's having Margaret picking at me, trying to find out everything I've ever done or thought or said."

"You know Margaret would be pleased," Anna said. "She's always talking about why don't you have a girl, and all that."

"Just don't mention it," he said. "I don't mean I'm in *love,* or anything."

"Keith, why did you run away from school last year?" Anna said. "Did you have a girl then?"

"No," he said. "There wasn't anything to make me want to stay there then—not a girl or a friend or anything. And I hated it."

"But why?"

"You wouldn't understand," he said.

"Yes I would. Was it because they made you do a lot of things you didn't want to do?"

He looked sideways at her. "You can't be by yourself," he said. "You can't get your breath. I *have* to be by myself sometimes. And there isn't any . . . *country.* After a while you feel . . . crazy. All those kids are there every minute, day and night. You can't get away from them." He was silent a minute. Then, "They're so stupid, Anna," he said. "Dumb, rich babies." He spoke thoughtfully, as if half to himself. "That may sound conceited, but it's true. They don't know the things we know."

"Do we know something special?" she said in a wondering voice.

"Don't you think we're kind of born old?" he said. "Yes," he answered himself. "I saw things, knew things, the day I was born that they'll never know, and so did you, and if you don't see that, you're a fool."

"Do you think *he* knows all those things you're talking about?"

she asked, pointing to The Count, who was walking some yards ahead of them.

"Oh, The Count!" Keith laughed indulgently. "He's a big operator," he said. "He's got his own kind of knowledge."

"It seems to me he's got his own kind of no-knowledge."

"Maybe no-knowledge is what I need," Keith said. "But what I was talking about before," he went on, "about having a girl and so on, I had a special reason for telling you."

"What?"

"Well, I thought it might make you feel better about having me around for a few days."

Anna was baffled. She could think of nothing to say that would make sense as an answer to this curious statement.

"I mean you can be my . . ." he hesitated, and then went on, "my confidante. I'll tell you all about it." He looked down at her, walking beside him along the shady street, trying to match her steps to his long stride, and smiled. "You don't have to be so unhappy," he said. "Come on, I'll help you tough it out. You might as well let me, because it looks like you're going to be stuck with me as long as The Count and Caroline . . ." He broke off. "Honestly, next year you'll probably wonder what in the world it was you were so unhappy about," he said.

She could scarcely believe that he had seen her misery. Her eyes filled with tears of gratitude. "I don't mind being stuck with you," she said. "I'd a lot rather . . ." She had been about to say, "I'd a lot rather be stuck with you than with him," when she had thought that after all he *was* Keith's best friend.

Keith laughed. "You're a real diplomat, sweetie," he said. "You'll go far."

"Maybe they'd like to go to the country—out to Selina's," Anna said hopefully. "We could have a picnic. Selina told us last week there's a pretty good swimming hole in the bayou this year."

"Why not?"

"Tété and Clarence could take us out there."

He turned on her with an intensity that startled her. "For crying out loud, Anna, grow up," he said. "I can drive a car. Tété and Clarence don't need to take us."

That Saturday night there was a dance at The Silver Cat, a nightclub a few miles outside Homochitto. A "name band" was playing, and the dance had been advertised over the radio and in the Homochitto *News* every day for weeks. Friday afternoon The Count suggested that they go.

Caroline immediately said, no, she had never been to a nightclub and was sure her mother would not approve.

"We don't have to ask her, do we?" The Count said. "We could tell her we were going to the show. Isn't there a midnight show on Saturday? That way, we could stay pretty late."

"My gosh, Count," Caroline said. "Everybody in town will be out there. Somebody would see us and tell Margaret."

"Why should anybody tell her? They'd think she already knew."

"Uh-*huh*."

"Come on, Keith, let's go. We'd have a good time."

Keith made an effort toward boredom. "We don't want to take these *kids* to a nightclub," he said.

"Scared you'll get in trouble?"

"Hell, no." Keith, sprawled out on the big couch in the south parlor, shifted uneasily in his place, and then sat up.

"Well, why not then? Just for kicks."

"In the first place," Keith said, lying without thought, "Margaret wouldn't mind if we took them—I mean, as long as I'm along. I just think it would be a bore."

"Music, boy! Lights! Whiskey! And so forth."

Keith, forced into a dilemma that the friendship had after all invited, looked at The Count as intently as if he had just materialized from nothing in the dim, shuttered parlor, and as if he found the sight both surprising and unattractive. The Count, sitting on the arm of the sofa next to Caroline, reached down and took her hand in his. His small, close-set eyes gleamed with blind, self-absorbed pleasure, as if he were listening to distant music, and he brought Caroline's hand up and rubbed it against his cheek.

Keith stood up, and, turning his back on them, stared out of the window.

"Well?"

"I'm not much in favor," Keith said.

The subject was dropped, but the next afternoon, the day of the dance, The Count brought it up again. "Come on, boy," he said to Keith. "Humor the old Count. Let's do it, huh? Nobody'll know the difference."

"It wouldn't be any fun," Keith said. "The high-school crowd doesn't go to The Silver Cat."

It was obvious to Anna that he did not want to take Caroline without asking, and that he would rather do anything than ask, and it was also clear that The Count (Stupid! she said to herself) had not the faintest notion of the danger he was pushing them into, a danger which she herself sensed with every nerve end, but could not put a name to.

"Who cares about any old two-bit high-school crowd?" The Count said. "Come on. Let daddy have his way."

"Where is Margaret?" Anna said.

Nobody answered her.

"We might have a good time," Caroline said, "but I'm not going without asking Margaret or Tété!"

"Tété!" The Count said. "You mean you ask that old woman what you can do?"

Caroline frowned at him. "I told you not to talk about Tété," she said.

"All *right*," Keith said. "All *right*. Go on, Caroline. Ask Margaret, if you've got to be so good."

But when Caroline went to talk with her mother, she found that Margaret had gone across the river to an all-afternoon and evening card party at a friend's cabin on the lake. She sought out Tété, who was busy in the kitchen supervising preparations for the dinner hour at the tearoom.

"No!" Tété said, as soon as she heard what The Count wanted to do. "You know you can't go to that Silver Cat. I never heard of no decent young girl going to that Silver Cat."

"But Tété, Clyde McCoy is playing."

"I never heard of no Clyde McCoy, and neither would you have, if it wasn't for *him*."

"Him who?"

"You know who I mean. That Count."

When Caroline reported that Tété had refused permission, Keith immediately reversed himself. "We could sneak off," he said. "Nobody would know the difference."

"Sneak off from a *nurse?*" The Count muttered to Anna in a low voice.

Anna pretended not to hear him. "Y'all can do what you want to, but I'm not going," she said.

"Come on, don't be a wet blanket," The Count said.

"Come on," Caroline said. "It'll be fun."

Anna shook her head stubbornly.

"You're getting mighty self-righteous, sweetie," Keith said.

"Who'll be Keith's date?" Caroline said.

"I don't care who he takes. I'm not going, that's all. I don't want to go and I'm not going."

"Let her alone," The Count said. "We can still go."

Anna picked up a book and pretended to read while the others made their arrangements. They would wait until Tété, who always went to bed by eight-thirty, had settled down, and then they would pretend to go to their rooms. But they would dress instead and sneak back downstairs, go to the Cat for a couple of hours and be home before Margaret got back from the lake. They *must* go. When would they have a chance again to hear a band like Clyde McCoy's?

They did just what they had planned. Anna, after she had helped Caroline dress, slipped down the stairs in her robe to watch them leave, and sat below the stair landing, peering after them through the banisters. A night-light, gleaming faintly in one of the wall sconces in the hall, threw their shadows behind them. The heavy curving legs of the mahogany pier stand loomed out of the semi-darkness; above the pier stand a tall mirror hung, and Anna watched the three shadowy figures move like phantoms across its surface. On either side of the mirror, along the walls, varnish-darkened portraits looked down as if through depths of murky water.

Whispering and giggling, Caroline and the two boys tiptoed toward the front door.

Tété's certainly going to hear them, if they keep on making so much noise, Anna thought. They must be crazy. Her stomach muscles knotted with anxiety.

In some curious way this harmless escapade had grown in her

mind until it had lost all connection with reality. Briefly she remembered an occasion, two or three years earlier, when she had sneaked off with her older sister and gone to a forbidden movie. It had been Lon Chaney in *The Unholy Three*—the very title a promise of initiation into depths of evil, the reality of which she did not doubt, but the concrete circumstances of which somehow always failed to materialize. They had gone to the movie. The story now had vanished from her mind as completely as if she had never seen it. The memory of her guilt, however, was as real as if it had been yesterday. She had lived with the guilt for days, and then had gone to her sister and said, "I can't help it, I've got to tell Mama." Her sister had known without explanation what she was talking about and had shrugged, her long serious face a mask of sophisticated boredom. "Tell her, then," she said. "I don't care. *Baby.*" Anna had confessed, expecting a punishment commensurate with her feeling of guilt, but nothing had happened. "Well, it's done," her mother had said. "I don't reckon it hurt you."

The memory of that week of pain, of the uncontrollable pangs of conscience, was perhaps what had kept her from going with Caroline tonight. But now she saw that it didn't matter whether you went or not. You still suffered. She felt as guilty as if she were involved, perhaps more so, for even though she stayed behind, she *was* involved, and now she was guilty as well of having been too cowardly to go along.

"Shh," she whispered to herself. "Be quiet, for goodness' sake."

"Shh," she heard The Count whisper. He squeezed Keith's arm. "For Christ's sake, shut up."

Keith had the car keys in his hand, and as he jerked away from The Count, he dropped them with a clatter that sounded as loud to Anna as the striking of the town clock.

They stood in the middle of the hall listening for a moment, and then tiptoed on. Anna watched, gripping the banisters with sweaty hands, listening to the silent house. They were even with the door to Tété's room, and, just after they passed it, it opened. There she stood, blocking the light from her doorway, dressed in an old gray flannel bathrobe. The thin black sticks of her legs, always hidden in the daytime, were visible halfway to the knees. On her feet were a pair of Margaret's discarded satin mules, and a black kerchief was tied around her head.

"It's nothing," Anna said to herself. "It's nothing but a silly dance, that's all, and now they can't go, and who cares? And she probably won't even tell Margaret. And if she did, Margaret would just laugh."

Then, for the space of a second, looking at Tété's feet in Margaret's satin mules, she saw the man in *The Unholy Three* who had masked his evil-doing behind a lace cap and long skirts, his ugly face distorted with arrogance and pride in his skill at dissembling.

She looks like an old witch peering out of her cave, Anna thought. And they're ghosts she's conjured up.

The two boys, their summer-tanned faces dark in the faint light, their white linen suits gleaming, might have been dark, white-draped ghosts, while Caroline, in a pale blue chiffon evening dress, loomed over Tété like a wispy floating giant.

"I reckon y'all think you're going to that dance," Tété said.

"Uh-huh," Keith said. "We are."

"*You* may be going," she said, "but you ain't taking my baby."

"Excuse me," The Count said with exaggerated hauteur, "if Mrs. Baird were here, I'm sure she would let Caroline go with us." He started for the door.

"Come on, Tété," Caroline said. "Please."

Tété walked a few steps down the hall to the front door and blocked their way. "If Sweet wants you to go," she said, "she ain't mentioned it to me."

"*Tété,*" Keith said.

The Count stared at Keith and Caroline. "She's nothing but a nigger maid," he said. "You're not going to pay any attention to her, are you?"

It's just a silly old dance, Anna said to herself again. For crying out loud, who cares about a silly old dance. But now she had a word to attach her guilt to; the senseless storm of emotion had a center. She drew herself together, brought her knees up to her chin, and wrapped her arms around them. I *hate* him, she thought. I *hate* him.

No one answered The Count.

"Mr. Keith," Tété said. "I'm not speaking to you and Mr. Kimbrough. But I'm in charge of Caroline, and she's not going to no nightclub, unless you shove me out the way and take her."

The Count looked at Keith and then looked up at the ceiling, put his hands in his pockets and began to whistle through his teeth.

"Tété," Keith said, "go on to bed. Hear? Go on to bed."

The Count continued to whistle. Keith turned to him. "Knock that off, will you?" he said in a low even voice. "What do you know about it? What do you know about *anything*?"

Caroline looked frightened. "I guess Tété's right, Keith," she said. "I don't believe Margaret would really like me to go. I better not. Y'all go without me."

"For God's *sake,*" The Count muttered, as if to himself.

"*Tété,*" Keith said again.

She shook her head stubbornly. "No, sir," she said, giving the "sir" the inflection a servant uses with a strange guest in the house.

Keith stood perfectly rigid, his shoulders hunched as if to ward off a blow, motionless except that he kept opening and closing his hands where they hung by his sides. At last, "I'm going . . ." he said in a choked voice, "I have to go . . ." and he did push Tété aside, jerk open the door, and stride out of the house.

They all heard him clattering down the front steps.

Tété stood for a few seconds watching Caroline, whose eyes had filled with tears. "Ne' min', Baby," she said. "He'll be back in a little bit." Then she turned away and went back to her room.

"He always goes off like that when he gets mad," Caroline said to The Count. Her voice sounded strangely loud in the silent hall.

"I just wanted to show you a good time," The Count said. He shrugged and made an embarrassed face. "I'm sorry."

Caroline looked at him for a moment and then drew a deep breath, as if bringing herself to the point of speaking out. But she changed her mind. "It's all right," she said. "Forget it."

Anna got up and came down the steps. "We could play cards a while, till he comes home," she said. "Cribbage or rummy or something."

But he did not come back. No more than half an hour passed before the doorbell rang. Caroline went to the door, opened it, and found Charlotte McGovern standing there.

"Is your mother here, my dear?" Charlotte said. And then, looking at Caroline's dress, "Were you going to a *party?*" as if such an idea were preposterous.

"No'm," Caroline said. "We just . . ."

"Is your mother here?"

"She's gone to the lake to play cards," Caroline said. "She'll be back pretty soon."

"Let me come in," Charlotte said, for Caroline was standing in the doorway. Her expression was so strange that Caroline said, "Is something the matter, Charlotte? What is it?" still not moving out of the door.

"Let me come in, my dear." Charlotte took her arm and gently steered her into the hall. "Yes," she said. "You'd better call Tété. And . . . Clarence, I suppose. He can drive me over . . . No, I'll call him . . ."

"*What's the matter?*" Caroline said.

"There's been a wreck," Charlotte said. "Keith . . ."

He was not dead. The doctor who had received him at the emergency room of the hospital, a cousin to both the Bairds and the McGoverns, had called Charlotte to ask her to break the news to Margaret and bring her to the hospital.

It was one of those senseless accidents that no one could have foretold or prevented. Apparently Keith, still in a rage, had gotten into the old Cadillac and driven off northward along the winding road that follows the curves of the bluff. He *was* going too fast; the skid marks in the gravel showed that. It might not have been so serious, if he had been going slower. About two miles from town something had happened to the steering mechanism. The police investigation afterwards indicated that it had given way. He must have felt it going, have seen that the car was headed off the bluff. As they pieced it together later, it appeared that he had struggled to turn the car the other way, and had in fact turned it somewhat before he lost control. He had slammed on the brakes and, skidding sideways down the road, had crashed into the concrete abutment of a bridge across the bayou that cut down through the bluff just at that point.

If the bridge had not been there, he would certainly have gone off the bluff.

Keith never recovered from the accident. His skull had been frac-tured, crushed, and the brain damage was such that he was in a coma for weeks. Afterwards, although a partial regeneration of the brain tissue occurred, he was like a child. An injury to his spinal cord resulted in total paralysis of his lower limbs.

The following summer, when the McGoverns came to Homo-chitto, he was in a wheelchair.

He would sit for hours in the court between the garçonnières with his old clay ocarina in his hands. He turned it over and over, and sometimes looked at it wonderingly and lifting it to his lips, blew gently into it, a questioning series of notes. Then he would look at it again for a long time, as if he had spoken to it and were waiting for an answer. He could not play a whole tune.

Now and then Tété would come slowly out of the tearoom or the house, moving more painfully now, the vigorous thump of her walk slowed by rheumatism, her hands hanging gnarled and knotty by her sides. She would look at him for a long time, and sometimes would come over and fan away a fly or mosquito buzzing around his head. In June, Margaret screened in part of the lower gallery of the garçon-nière to protect him from insects.

In the morning and again in the afternoon, while the tearoom was closed, Clarence, dressed in a dark chauffeur's uniform and a stiff-billed cap, would take him for long strolls, pushing the chair and keeping up a patter of conversation as he walked. Keith nodded and smiled, and every now and then, with a queer, guttural crow of joy, pointed out to Clarence a flying bird, a dog, or a towboat steam-

ing slowly upriver with a string of barges. He seemed quite happy.

Caroline spent a great deal of time with him too, making cats' cradles of twine, or cutting out strings of dancing paper dolls to amuse him, playing records for him on the Victrola. For a long time, although the doctors had said it was useless, she tried to teach him to be himself. She put the guitar in his hands and showed him again and again where to put his fingers on the frets. She read aloud to him from simple children's books, pointing to the words as she read, and trying to get him to say them. She talked to him every day of what he had loved—the woods, the river, and his books—watching his face and demanding a response: Do you remember, Keith? Do you see? The patience and resolution in her thin face were all the more pitiful because of her youth; for she was still hardly more than a child.

Later, when she read to him, it was from whatever book she happened to be reading herself. He smiled while she read and turned the ocarina over in his hands and sometimes blew into it.

Caroline withdrew more and more that year from the company of her contemporaries, and now it was Anna who tried to coax her out to swim, to the movies, to a party, or on a double date. Usually she would not come, and when she did, she was so quiet the boy did not ask her for another date.

The following two summers Anna and Caroline saw almost nothing of each other. Anna was a junior counselor at a summer camp one year, and the next she went to summer school to pick up a couple of extra courses before going off to college. The backwards letters had of course stopped with the end of childhood, and, although they exchanged Christmas presents, they almost never wrote to each other. It was as if Keith sat between them, smiling his mindless smile. To see each other, to speak, they had to peer around him, and then after all there was nothing to say.

The winter Caroline was eighteen, Keith died of a severe kidney infection. Everyone in Homochitto agreed that it was a blessing not only for the Baird family, but for the poor, broken boy himself, that God had taken him.

Anna was a freshman in college that year and Caroline, who had not started school until she was seven, was a senior in high school. Charlotte wrote Anna of Keith's death, and Anna sat down immediately and wrote Caroline a long letter, a summation of all that their childhood friendship had meant to her—the joy of summer days, the very, bitter-sweet beginnings of their lives. She could scarcely bear to mention Keith's name in her letter, so cruel did his death seem, so clearly did she feel the horror of life snatched away before it could be begun. "I don't want to die," she said to herself. "I don't want to die, *ever*."

The only answer she received was an engraved card: "The family of Keith Baird . . ."

A few weeks later Charlotte wrote that Margaret had taken Caroline out of school. Or rather, that Caroline had gotten up one morning and refused to leave the house.

It was shortly after this that Anna received a letter from Caroline, the first in more than a year.

We've always lived on the bluff, you know that. [It began abruptly, without salutation.] *One can expect a slide.* [Here the ink changed color, as if the letter had been abandoned and later begun again.] *When we were warriors and princesses, a long time ago, when I was a captive of the Saracens—do you remember that? Did you ever think that stories had happy endings? Well, they don't. No, there is no form to them, no one thing that makes the characters act—everything is confusion, and, when endings come, they are not endings for you but only fear, or fury, or despair, or death for someone else, and for you, bewilderment, and grief that doesn't end at all, but lodges in your bones, that gets up with you in the morning and goes to bed with you at night and twists your dreams in knots; and that doesn't end either, but goes on, goes on, goes on, until maybe if you're lucky you find you're someone else and already in the middle of another story.*

Again the letter broke off and the last part was written in a big, hasty pencil scrawl:

Can anything be done can anything be done can anything be done. We're all here and the house all around walls and glass. Broken. And at last after all he *was the one who—She* hung on, *all strong hands and will—and he fell—broken—slides—yes, falling, yes—Oh, cruel. . .*

It broke off.

With icy hands and feet, trembling so with distress that she could scarcely hold a pen, Anna sat down and wrote a letter to her mother, enclosing Caroline's letter to her.

It's all their fault, Mama, [she wrote in a passion of sorrow and resentment]. *It's all their fault from the beginning, Margaret's and Tété's. And it's their fault, too, about Keith—poor, poor Keith.* [She began to weep, and wrote on, brushing away her tears.] *No one cared enough. How is it possible for things to be so gay and perfect on the surface, and underneath, all the time, such terrible trouble?*

Keith was too good, that's all. Yes, the only thing wrong with him was he was good. *The better you are and the more intelligent you are, the worse things will go with you—that's plain enough. You see, like he did, yourself and everybody else, and it drives you out, just like it drove him out. While somebody like that awful John Kimbrough can go through life as innocent as a baby—not ever guilty of all the terrible things he does and causes.*

[And then,] *I don't know what to do about this, that's why I'm sending it to you. Do you think Margaret ought to know about it?* [Then,] *No, don't show it to Margaret. Caroline would never forgive me, I know, if her mother or Tété saw it. But what shall I do?*

Charlotte wrote back:

Get hold of yourself, my dear. Keith had a wreck, *an automobile accident. It was not Margaret's fault or Tété's or even John Kimbrough's. It was an accident. No one could possibly have known that the steering mechanism on that old car would give way.*

As for the letter you sent me, I think you are right. You should not send it to Margaret. M. is living in the house with Caroline; she sees her every day. Nothing that you or I could say would add to her understanding of her. It is best for us not to interfere. As for you, I think you can write to Caroline and say whatever your heart prompts you to say. And pray, *as we all must, for her, for them, for us all.*

V

CIRCUMSTANCES kept Anna and Caroline apart during the years that followed Keith's death, brought a virtual end to their friendship through the simple fact of separation.

Caroline married quite young. She must have found within herself some resource with which to confront the fact of her brother's death, for shortly after Anna received that one letter from her, she went back to school, completed her final term, and graduated. But she did not go away to finishing school as Margaret had hoped she would or give her mother the vicarious pleasure of a gay girlhood. Instead, the summer of 1939, after her graduation, she fell in love with one of her mother's "gentleman roomers," Thomas Carter, a young geologist who had come to Homochitto with an oil exploration team for one of the big oil companies. The following winter she married him.

Anna met him briefly the summer before the wedding; but she stayed only a couple of days in Homochitto that year, for she had a summer job that kept her at home until just before school started in the fall. During the few hours that she and Caroline were together, they talked of Anna's school, of Caroline's love affair, of the future; but they did not speak of the past.

In November 1940 the National Guard unit of which Thomas was a member was called up, and Caroline left Homochitto to be gone, except for an occasional short visit, until after the end of the Second World War. Anna was away at college, then working, and then married; and so it happened that the two girls did not see each other again until 1946.

Of course, during that time, Anna saw the Bairds. Whenever she was in Homochitto, she went punctiliously to call. She found them always the same, or so it seemed to her—Tété a bit more rheumatic, perhaps, and Margaret beginning at last to show her age. She still touched up her hair, and its shining blackness brought out every wrinkle on her aging face. But she had all her old charm, a charm that to Anna seemed now to say, almost frantically, "Nothing has happened. Everything is grand."

All through the war Margaret kept the house crowded with young men. She was chairman of the dance committee for the local USO, and lonely soldiers from the nearby army camp clustered around her like freezing men around a campfire. But the wind was at their backs; they came and then vanished into the war, as if they had never been there.

Anna, when she came to call, listened to Margaret's accounts of their troubles and adventures and then, as always, asked about Caroline.

"I don't see how she does it," Margaret said. "It's absolutely beyond me. In fact, you young people have left me behind. There she is, out in Kansas, in the middle of nowhere, not a servant to be had for gold, with two babies, and it doesn't seem to bother her one bit. I begged her to come home to have this last one—we could make things so easy for her here. But no, nothing would do but she must stay out there with Thomas. You'd think Thomas would *insist* on her coming home. Why, she had to hop out of bed and go to work practically the minute Peggy was born—just like a field hand. Didn't she, Tété?"

Tété nodded. "'Tain't right," she said. "She going to ruin herself."

"Tété wanted to go out there and stay with them," Margaret said, "rheumatism or no rheumatism, but Caroline said it would be too much for her, and of course she was right.

"Oh, I went and helped out for a couple of weeks—but you know, she packed me off just as soon as she politely could. Said she could manage by herself. And the truth is, she has the strength of an army. She *could* manage by herself." Margaret shook her head. "When I was young, a woman had a practical nurse for at least six weeks after a baby. She didn't have to lift a finger. And she pampered herself for six months, or even longer than that if she was frail."

The summer of 1946, after her own marriage, Anna stopped overnight in Homochitto. She was on her way from her home in the little Delta town of Philippi for a visit with her parents in Eureka, and had with her her son, born the preceding winter. As soon as she had seen her kin and heard about the comings and goings of aunts and uncles and cousins, she went to see the Bairds. Caroline was home at last, and this time, apparently, to stay.

The opening of the famous Homochitto oil field, during the last year of the war, had brought in several of the big oil companies, and Caroline's husband Thomas, coming back to his job after the war, had moved up in his company's hierarchy to a minor executive position, and been put in charge of its Homochitto office. After some months spent in New York, at the company's executive training school, he had brought his family South. At Margaret's invitation, they had moved, only a few weeks before Anna's visit, into the Baird house garçonnière.

Margaret now had a substantial income from oil royalties on her own farm land, land she had managed to hold onto all through the Depression, although everyone at the time had said it was worthless. She had closed the tearoom, asked several of her roomers to move, and turned over the north wing of the garçonnière to the young family. She had even partitioned the tearoom and made a kitchen out of one end, so that the Carters and their children could have a wholly independent household.

In the south wing, her three favorite roomers still lived.

"I couldn't bear to make them all leave," she told Anna that evening. "I've gotten so *attached* to them. And it's always nice at five o'clock to be sure there'll be someone around to have a drink with. You get lonesome."

"You shouldn't get lonesome any more," Anna said, "with all this crowd."

Sitting in the screened-in end of the garçonnière gallery where Keith had used to sit in his wheel chair, they were surrounded by children. Anna's baby and Caroline's youngest lay kicking and gurgling in buggies close by, and Caroline's two older children, Tom, five, and Peggy, three, trotted in and out, still absorbed in their exploration of their new home.

"Well, I must say, they're not much good to me at the cocktail hour," Margaret said. "That's the most frantic time of the day for Caroline."

It was seven o'clock in the evening, the magic hour of a southern summer day. Against the deep blue twilight sky the upper branches of the live oak tree in the court swayed to the touch of a breeze off the river. Swifts soared and darted in the clear air; invisible locusts called harshly to each other, one far away, another answering start-lingly from just outside the gallery.

Anna and Caroline had spent the afternoon together. They had no difficulty becoming friends again; as sometimes happens, after a few tentative forays into each other's lives, they established an easy rapport and were comfortable.

Perhaps this ease resulted not so much from their common past as from their common obsessions. For both of them, as Anna recognized immediately, were immersed in the peculiarly female absorption of the early years of marriage—an interior life almost wholly occupied with sex—with voluptuous daydreams, and at night with the eventful private world of the flesh, with pregnancy and childbirth, with their passionate concern for the small, struggling, helpless, maddeningly irritating children who possess a young woman's life.

They did not, of course, talk of sex, for they were not women who could speak of making love as if it were golf or canasta; they talked instead first of old times, then of books, and finally of their husbands and children. Now the older children had been fed; Anna's baby grunted, dozed, burrowed, and fell asleep in the buggy. Caroline's, a small blond boy whom she had named for Keith, began to fret, and she took him up and sat down in a low rocker to nurse him. As Anna watched, she said to herself that nothing was left of the old Caroline, the child who had hidden in the laurel tree, the thin tormented girl who had read aloud to Keith in his wheelchair, nothing except the shy, loving expression in her blue eyes, the intelligent, ironic lift of her dark brows. Her figure now was heavy and matronly, her face, carelessly made up, was quiet and passive as she nursed the child.

"Babies!" Margaret said. "I believe she intends to repopulate the world."

Caroline shifted her breast, beautifully swelling and white, heavy with milk, and eased the baby's greedy pulling at it. "We can't get along without a baby," she said. "We have to have a little one, a *tiny* one."

"*Indefinitely?*"

"Well . . ." She smiled at her mother and said no more.

For a little while they talked desultorily of this and that, and Anna was getting ready to gather her belongings to go when they heard the back door of the big house close, and Tété's heavy tread crossing the court toward them. She came onto the gallery, shooing Peggy, Caroline's three-year-old, ahead of her.

Anna, who had not yet greeted the old woman, rose and received the ceremonious kiss of welcome. Then Tété turned to Caroline.

"This child was out on the front gallery, getting ready to go down the steps," she said. "We got to keep the door locked."

Peggy crossed the gallery and leaned against her mother's side, staring fixedly down at her baby brother. Caroline gathered the child against her with one arm, while she still held the baby with the other.

"She knows not to go in the street, Tété. She's a city girl. And you forget, she's never had anyone to watch her all the time. I've taught her to stay where she belongs." Caroline rose and put the now sleeping baby in his buggy. Then she sat down again and took Peggy on her lap. "Sit down with us a little while," she said to Tété. "You and Anna haven't had a visit for years."

"Miss Anna, you looking fine." The old woman lowered herself painfully into a chair.

"You haven't seen *my* baby," Anna said. She rolled the buggy close to Tété's chair, and Tété peered in, her lower lip thrust out in judicious approval, her seamed face serious.

"Ain't he fine! But you got to go far to catch up with us." She cackled delightedly, the laugh of extreme old age, so unlike her that Anna glanced up, startled.

Tété pulled back the light throw for a closer inspection. "You got a large child," she said. "Is his daddy big?"

Anna nodded. "Six-two."

"He's wet."

"I see he is," Anna said. "But he's sleeping. I don't want to bother him."

Tété raised her clawlike hands and held them out for Anna to inspect. "No good," she said. "I'm no good to Caroline with these. Can't even pin on a didy."

"I know you can still play checkers," Anna said. "It won't be long before Tom and Peggy will be old enough to take you on."

Tété looked sharply out at her from behind the mask of age and debility, and Anna recognized at once the old uncompromising realism that declined the small subterfuges of courtesy, and was disappointed when you offered them.

"Hmmmph," Tété said.

"Did you see Tom in the house, Tété?" Caroline said. "He wandered off in your direction right after supper."

"Last I saw him he asked me could he go see what was in the storeroom, and I told him it was all right." Tété nodded toward the wing across the court. "I heard him in there when I come out," she said.

Margaret rose. "I'm going in the house and get some whiskey," she said. "We can all have a drink. Isn't that a good idea? Tété, I'll bring you a drop of sherry."

"No'm, thank you," Tété said. "I'll just set here a minute and then go. I mainly wanted to bring this child to Caroline and tell her she was out on the front porch."

"Thomas will be home in a few minutes," Caroline said. "He can fix us all a drink, Mama. You don't need to get yours. Or I can fix us one, as soon as I settle the children down."

"Let me," Margaret said. "I'll do it while you're putting the children to bed."

"I suppose I really ought to go," Anna said. "It's getting late."

"No indeed. You've got to stay and see Thomas."

They heard a door close on the other side of the court, and the light, sure footsteps of a child approaching.

"Tom?" Caroline called. "Come on in, it's bedtime."

The child bumped against the screen door, opened it with his shoulder, and backed through, carrying something in both arms; then he turned around. Anna caught her breath. In the fading light he might have been Keith. His face was flushed and rosy with exertion, a smear of cobwebs across his dark hair and down one cheek, his slanting green eyes shining with delight. He carried in his arms— its fat curving body larger than his own—Keith's old guitar.

"Mama! Look what I found in the storeroom. Look! May I have it? Can it be mine?"

No one said anything for a moment.

Then, "We'll see, darling," Caroline said. "We'll put it up and see in the morning." She got up. "It's time for you two to be in bed."

Tété peered through the gathering darkness. "What's he got?" she said. "Ain't nothing in that storeroom worth anything."

He crossed the room to her, still carrying the guitar, and put it in her lap. "Look, Tété!" he said. "I found it in a trunk, way down under everything. Is it yours? Can I have it? *Please.*"

She did not answer him.

"*Please*," he said. "*Please.*"

"Keith?" Tété said.

"I'm not Keith. I'm Tom. Keith is a *baby.*"

The old woman put her crippled hands on the guitar to keep it from sliding off her lap, and stared down at it. "Keith?" she said.

Leading Peggy, Caroline crossed the gallery and tried to take the guitar from her. "I'll put it away until tomorrow," she said again.

But Tété did not let go. Instead she turned to Margaret. "Do you remember when we got it, Sweet?"

Margaret had half risen from her chair. Now she sank back and nodded. "Yes," she said.

The harsh cries of the locusts rose and fell from tree to tree, loud in the quiet dusk.

"Do *you* remember?" Tété asked Anna.

"I—I don't think so. I remember the summer he was first learning to play it, and how he used to sing, 'M' Yalla, Oh, M' Yalla, Oh, M'Yalla Gal.'" Anna smiled uncertainly.

"It was the year we started the tearoom," Tété said. "When everybody was poor. That was the year we got it, and Keith got tired of the sweet potato that year, and he had to have a guitar. He *had* to have one, that was all, and Sweet knew it and I knew it and we got him one. There wasn't no money and it cost thirty-five dollars and Sweet got it. I don't know how she got it, she probably didn't know herself." She spoke in an expressionless voice, looking down at the guitar.

There was nothing to say in reply; the silence of grief, of love's bitter failures, fell upon them all.

At last, "The children have to go to bed," Caroline said. "Tom, Peggy, tell Sweet and Tété goodnight." She stepped inside the house and turned on the gallery light. "You all are sitting in the dark," she said, and then, gently, "Come on, Tété, let me put the guitar away."

As Tété gave it up, there passed across her face for an instant such a look of desolation as Anna had never seen or imagined possible.

"Come on, Tété," Margaret said. "It *is* dark. I'll help you back to the house."

Tété stood up and took one heavy step toward Margaret, who rose at the same time to help her.

"Sweet?" Tété said. And then, in a low voice, hardly more than a whisper, "He's dead. Our beautiful child is dead."

Tété, too, is dead now, in the fullness of her years. Margaret buried her in the Baird family plot in the Homochitto cemetery, under the blue-green cedar trees. The stone at her head reads:

Theresa Howard
"Tété"
Born 1867   Died July 3, 1953
"Mine eyes shall be upon the
faithful of the land, that
they may dwell with me."

Margaret, and Caroline and her family still live in the house on the bluff. Thomas has left the oil company and has an excellent position with one of the new factories that moved into Homochitto after the war; people say he will eventually be head of it. There are two more children; the garçonnières echo to their voices, to the creak of swing chains and the careless slamming of doors.

Selina's granddaughter, Marie, has moved into town, and helps Caroline with the children. She has a family of her own and doesn't want to live in the big house; but Margaret has bought her a small cottage nearby, so she can get back and forth to work easily. Some days, when she has no one to leave her own baby with, Marie pushes him to work in his buggy, and he lies in the pleasant shade of the garçonnière gallery all morning.

With so many children to look after, Marie is a help. But Caroline still likes to do most things for her family herself. She has never been a "joiner," and she stays a great deal at home. She takes the children to the country, too, on picnics, or long walks, and points out the wild birds—field larks and mourning doves, cardinals, robins and mockingbirds, once or twice even a painted bunting.

"To find happiness in little things," she said shyly to Anna one summer day. "It sounds fancy, I reckon, but that's what I want for them. There's so much joy to be had in the world . . ."

Last year, so Charlotte wrote Anna, there was a small slide on the bluff just south of the Baird house. Fortunately, no one was hurt. Friends have advised the family to sell, but it's hard to find a buyer in that dangerous neighborhood. And then, there are advantages—the sunsets, the view of the river. And besides, their investment in the property, the years they've spent there—all these things make it hard to pull up stakes and move. Margaret says they'll probably stay on, at least as long as Caroline and Thomas are willing.

Jesse
(Philippi)

WHEN WE KNEW HIM, Jesse Daniels was already an old man. He had been draft age during the First World War, and had gone to France.

"I couldn't take my fiddle to the war with me," he told me, when we were talking about his travels one day, "but I took my Jew's harp and my sweet potato. I was already a good fiddler at that time, and a good drummer, too. Music come easy to me. I played with Louis Armstrong in New Orleans, 1915, 1916." He paused and looked at me as if to see if I was impressed.

"Louis Armstrong!" I said. "Did you really?"

He nodded. "Then I got drafted," he said, "and when I come back to New Orleans after the war, all that old gang was busted up, kind of, some gone one way and some the other. I played here and there—Vicksburg, Natchez, Homochitto, out to Texas, up to Chicago. I never liked Chicago and all them places much. Too cold. And no fishing to speak of. I'd play up there in the spring and summer some years and then come back here to Philippi in the winter. A man can make out in Philippi. Plant him a patch of greens, fish, get him up a little band. I always got two or three boys here willing to go in on a band with me, and we could make enough to live. Nowadays, though, it's even better. You get your unemployment every year a long time—some years I get it twenty or more weeks; and then when you get up my age you got your social security. So now I don't have to play nowhere if I don't want to. I had a job out to Minnesota two, three years before my social security come in, playing concerts at a—a— you know what I'm talking about, Miss, one of them old peoples . . ."

"An old people's home?" I asked.

"That's it," he said. "Nothing but old peoples. And they treat 'em so nice. They got the best of all kinds of food, and they got radios and TVs, everything. And they kept us on a long time just to play for 'em every night. They got beards."

"*What?*"

"Beards. Everyone of 'em, Miss. The men, I mean. Everyone of 'em got long beards. They don't let 'em cut 'em off. They some kind of special peoples. You know what I mean? They belongs to something or other special. Some kind of a house they calls it."

"Oh," I said. "Is it the House of David?"

"That's it, Miss. That's where they keeps they old folks. It was a good job—easy hours, steady work, good pay. But I'm glad to be home. I never did catch on to the fishing up there, and it seems to me the fishing down here gets better every year. I caught me around a hundred or more breams in Calloway's Blue Hole yesterday."

"Better not let the game warden hear about it," I said.

"No indeed, Miss. I sold half of 'em before I ever went home."

The first time I saw Jesse was the day I drove down to his house to interview him about teaching my son Ralph to play the guitar. We had heard of him from friends who had hired his little band to play at a party, and who knew that he gave guitar lessons. I had telephoned him to expect me, and following his directions, had driven slowly along Pearl Street until I found his house. A neat, three-room shotgun house with a small vine-covered porch, it was one of only two recently painted buildings in the block; the others were weathered to a uniform soft gray.

Very few of Philippi's respectable Negroes live on Pearl Street, particularly if they have children. It's a noisy neighborhood, the red-light houses sandwiched in between nightclubs like the Casablanca and the Live and Let Live; tumbledown fish markets, Chinese grocery stores, cafés and secondhand clothing and furniture stores crowded into a ten-block slum. But it was the right neighborhood for an old-time jazz musician, and I thought nothing of Jesse's living there.

His house was a block from the Casablanca, a huge rickety old dance hall with an unsavory reputation, and two blocks from what was rumored to be an integrated house of prostitution. But it was a sturdy house, the small porch clean, the yard, unlike the cluttered yards of neighboring houses, broom-marked where it had been recently swept. An old washtub by the front steps was full of white petunias.

Jesse was waiting for me on the front porch when I arrived. As he stood up and came toward the car, my heart sank. I didn't think he could possibly teach anyone anything. He was a scarecrow of a man, a great, tall, loose bundle of sticks with a shambling walk. His long arms and legs seemed to have a will of their own, moving somehow in unexpected directions; his gestures were outlandish, extravagant, as if his arms and hands didn't know what he was talking about and always thought he was telling a wild story. He looked, too, as if he had deliberately dressed himself as ridiculously as possible. He had on an old, battered felt hat turned inside out, the upside-down brim tilted at a dashing angle, and a pair of jeans six inches too short. The black sticks of his legs showed above his shoes, so thin at the ankles I could have put my thumb and forefinger around them. I got out of the car and introduced myself to him, while he took off his hat and bowed and wagged his head self-consciously.

But when he began to tell me about himself and to discuss the lessons, he relaxed, and his face had a certain amount of sober dignity and self-possession that were reassuring. His eyes were small and alert, his high, sloping forehead merged into a shining bald dome fringed with stiff, short black hair, he had a long jaw, deeply lined from nostrils to chin, and a wide, kind mouth. He apologized for the way he was dressed, saying he had just come in from fishing, and we made sensible arrangements about hours and prices.

"I got to see if the boy's got talent before I know can I teach him," he said. "I come the first time free."

The arrangement we made was for me to pick him up every Monday and Thursday afternoon and bring him to my house, and then to take him home afterward. He charged a dollar and a half a lesson. When he came out to get into the car the following week, the day of the first lesson, he wore a sensible, dark suit, and a respectable if ancient hat.

Jesse lived almost two miles from our house, and I spent considerable time alone with him that year, driving back and forth. That was how we happened to have so much conversation. When we got to the house, he was all business, going straight with Ralph to his room, closing the door, and setting to work. They laboriously tuned their guitars, and played over and over again three or four boogies, of which Ralph does not even remember the names, and "The St. Louis Blues," "Home on the Range," and "The Red River Valley." These songs apparently made up Jesse's whole repertoire—if he knew any others, he did not teach them to Ralph. Usually he did not sing the words to the songs, but hummed the tunes in his cracked old voice, interrupting himself now and then to call out the chord changes in the guitar accompaniment. Sometimes, in the course of a lesson, he would send Ralph out to borrow a cigarette from me; two or three times he came out himself, and in that case, at first, if I were having a drink or a can of beer, I would offer him one. But ordinarily, except for the faint sound of the guitars behind Ralph's closed door, I scarcely knew he was in the house.

Driving back and forth, Jesse and I talked a little about fishing or about Ralph's progress on the guitar, but mostly we talked about Jesse's life. Naturally, considering his age and profession, one of the first things I asked him was whether he had known Bud Scott, who was a famous old-time musician in our part of the country. I had heard him play when I was thirteen or fourteen, and had never forgotten it; he was coal black, enormously fat, and, when he sang, opened his huge mouth so that you could see all the cavernous red interior, and shouted out the words in a hoarse, raucous, gravelly voice that could be heard in the next county, even over the deafening, brassy tumult of his band. He died the year I heard him, but he had played for dances from St. Francisville to Greenville in my mother's day, and was one of our monuments, seeming, until he died, as indestructible as the Confederate soldier on his shaft in the courthouse yard. Jesse said, yes, he had known Bud well, in fact had played with him many times, and with his son Bud, Jr., who, after the old man died, had what nowadays they call a "combo." I remembered that Bud, Jr., had played the night of the Natchez fire, and Jesse told me he was in the combo at that time. It was during one of his out-of-work periods, when he had come South to regroup, so to speak.

The Natchez fire was in late spring 1939, and, except for the

1927 flood, it was the worst thing that ever happened in our part of the country. I suppose it has been forgotten everywhere else; so many people have been killed since 1939. But it will be a long time before our Negroes forget it. The dance was in a ramshackle night-club in Natchez, and all the colored young people in the county were there. The place was hung with Spanish moss, dry as tinder and flitted with some inflammable insecticide to get rid of the mosquitoes. Someone threw away a lighted match, or perhaps there was a spark of static electricity, no one ever knew exactly how it happened, but the place went off like a firecracker—exploded into flame. A few people near the front and back doors got out, but in the panic almost everyone was burned or suffocated or trampled to death—five hundred people. There was scarcely a Negro family in Natchez that didn't lose a child. Even in Philippi, a hundred miles away, we felt it. Everyone had connections with somebody who died in the Natchez fire.

Jesse told me that he just missed playing with Bud Scott, Jr., that night. At the time, he said, he had had a lady friend living in Ferriday, over the river from Natchez, and he was with her that day. She didn't want to go to the dance and persuaded Jesse to drive with her to Lake Providence instead, to visit her brother's family. He didn't even bother to get anyone in his place, he said. He didn't have that on his conscience. He just didn't show up. The next morning, getting up for breakfast, they heard about it on the radio. Bud Scott, Jr., and almost everyone in the band died in the fire.

Jesse told me he had been lucky like that all his life; even when he was living in Chicago during the twenties and thirties, playing in what must have been mostly dives and speakeasies, he had stayed out of trouble.

"How did you manage?" I asked. "Weren't you scared of all those gangsters up there?"

"Yes, *ma'am*, I was scared. You *got* to be scared. And you got to keep your money in your bosom. I know plenty men up there still sits with they back in a corner in the café—you know, where you can see the door and all—so nobody can sneak up on them. I had a friend up there wasn't scared, and he ended up in Lake Michigan with a concrete block to his feet. I warned him, too. I told him, 'You can get along fine up here if you keep your eyes and your mouth shut, and stay scared.' But he wanted to be a big man."

I asked Jesse once if he had ever heard the "Natchez Fire Blues" or the "Philippi Pearl Street Blues," and he told me he knew them, and knew the fellows who had written both of them. They are not good songs, only run-of-the-mill blues, or what we call "race music," the kind that is played on the local radio stations (or used to be before rock-and-roll came in) every afternoon from one until five to advertise hair straighteners. Jesse laughed when I asked him about the "Pearl Street Blues," and asked me if I had ever heard "Greenville Smokin', Leland Burnin' Down," written by the same fellow. I said I had never even heard *of* it, and he shrugged and said, well, they didn't play it on the radio, and he reckoned there were white men in Leland, Greenville too, who would think nothing of shooting any nigger they heard singing that song. I was curious, and two or three times afterward I tried to get him to play "Greenville Smokin', Leland Burnin' Down" for me on the guitar and sing it, but he never would. I even tried to get him to explain what he meant about the shooting part, and he seemed to try, but somehow he always got confused or got me confused. Once when I asked him about it, he said he didn't think the "bossman" would like it, and then I gave up. I realized that he did not want to assume anything, to take anything for granted. He was afraid of us.

I suppose people will wonder why it mattered to me, and sometimes I wonder myself; but I was troubled, and troubled people will grasp at any straw to vindicate themselves. It doesn't have to be anything that is important to anyone. I suppose, too, that my uneasiness is part of the reason we talked about the Natchez fire. I didn't want him to think I had dismissed it long ago, as so many white people have, as something that happened to a bunch of niggers.

He must have sensed what was going on in my mind, because one day, just before he got out of the car in front of my house, he said abruptly, for no reason that I could discover, "Miss, you such a good Christian, your daddy must be a preacher."

I knew he was trying to flatter me, to say what he thought would please, but even if he had been sincere, what could I have said in reply? That the churches are crowded every Sunday with his bitterest enemies? That I might not be what he would call "a Christian" at all?

"No," I said, "he's not a preacher, but he's an elder."

"I knew it," Jesse said. "I knew he was bound to be saved."

One more thing I'll say about wanting to make Jesse Daniels my friend. I have a passion for talking over old times, for hearing from old people how it was at such and such a time in such and such a place; and, particularly, if I can bring to bear anything out of my own recollections, can say, "That's right, of course, because I remember, or Gran told me something that fits right in with what you're saying." I like to hear my father tell how his father used to wad his old muzzle-loading shotgun with Spanish moss, aim it up into the holly tree in the front yard ("Right there—that's the tree") and bring down enough robins to have robin pie for dinner. More than anything I want to know *how it was*, to gather all the facts, and then to *understand*. For this reason it gave me a queer satisfaction to think of Jesse's driving to Lake Providence with his lady friend the day of the fire, sitting in the warm darkness on the little porch of her brother's house, laughing and drinking and slapping mosquitoes, going to bed and making love, and then getting up the next morning to hear the impersonal voice of the radio announcer describe the horror in which they had so nearly been consumed.

From the beginning, my husband did not care for Jesse. In the first place, Jesse wasn't much of a musician, and Richard thought we were throwing our money away. He was right, too. Jesse came twice a week for more than a year, and I don't believe he taught Ralph a dozen chords. I'll never forget how embarrassed I was for Jesse one afternoon after the lesson when I persuaded him to sit down at the piano in the living room and play and sing for us. Richard had come home early, and I thought I would give him a chance to judge Jesse for himself. Jesse was delighted to play. He put his greasy hat on top of the piano and, drawing up the chair, sat down and banged away at the keys as loudly as if he were playing in a crowded nightclub, and shouted out the words. But his scarred and knotty old fingers faltered, struck wrong notes, and could not even keep the time. We sat stiff-faced and silent until he finished and then praised him as enthusiastically as we could.

He knew how terrible he had sounded. "I got to have a couple of drinks to get going," he said, "and then, too, folks dancing and hollering, that limbers me up. I can't do no good cold." He got up and bowed and scraped his foot to Richard with exaggerated servility. "I try it for you again one day soon, Bossman," he went on. "I work up a coupla pieces good."

Richard looked as astonished and horrified as if someone had slapped him. Bossman, indeed! That was a little too much for him. And there was no reason, no excuse either of us could think of for servility. Richard had said nothing that could be interpreted as expecting or requiring it. Jesse just saw a white man and went into his act—like a firehorse at the clang of the alarm.

One reason he didn't see us more clearly, and another reason for Richard's disapproval of him, was that he was a heavy drinker. He had to use so much of his energy and intelligence trying to appear sober that he hadn't much left either for observing us or for teaching guitar. Even Ralph got to the place where he could tell whether Jesse had been drinking, and Ralph's experience with drinkers is negligible. After he told me two or three times that Jesse hadn't made sense again that afternoon, I had to tell Jesse not to come unless he was sober.

It didn't make much difference to him one way or the other. He made a good living. He taught guitar to half a dozen white children and piano to several Negro children. (It is hard to see how he kept his piano students, except that he was probably the only Negro piano teacher in Philippi.) He played almost every Friday and Saturday night at Negro dances and parties. He collected his social security, and his wife worked. He also "befriended" old people by helping them fill out forms for getting on the social security and the state old-age pension, charging twenty-five or fifty cents a person. He told me about this project one afternoon when I was driving him home— said he naturally felt sorry for old folks who didn't have any education, and wanted to do his part to help them. Of course, it is against the law to charge for such a service. I heard afterwards that the agent at the local Welfare Department threatened several times to have him prosecuted. But she never did anything about it, and Jesse continued to think of himself as a very charitable man. Somehow the fact never penetrated that the social workers at the Welfare Department would fill out the forms for nothing. Oh, he was an old scoundrel, all right. To do him justice, though, I know it's true that many of his "clients" may have been afraid to ask the workers to fill out their forms, or they may not have understood that they could, even if they had been told so when they applied for their pensions. Besides, some of the Negroes here think that the welfare agent has absolute power over the state's money and that she gives pensions to those she likes and withholds them from those who offend her; the caprices of the state legislature are always taken for her personal caprices, and it may even be that in the interest of her own prestige she encourages this misapprehension. Jesse's clients and perhaps even Jesse undoubtedly thought that a neatly filled-out form would help win the agent's favor.

Before many months of our acquaintance with Jesse had passed, I began to dread Ralph's guitar days. Sometimes it seemed to me that Jesse quite consciously tried to make me uncomfortable. A chance remark, a nervous laugh, an exaggerated gesture, and my afternoon was ruined. One day he told me how when he was a teen-age boy working for a white family in Natchez he had had to play horsey to the child in the house. "Man, that boy never got tired playing horse," he said. "Not till he got up practically grown. I can hear his maw now, when he was a boy big as Raff, 'Come on, Jesse. Johnny wants to play horse,' and I'd have to ride him till my knees shook. I'd ruther of picked a hundred pounds of cotton." There was something in his voice and manner that made me want to say, "But *I* had nothing to do with it."

"He does it deliberately," I told Richard that night. "He knows how to make us squirm. And besides that, it's gotten so I can't have a drink on Monday or Thursday afternoon until he's gone. If he's sober, I don't want to start him drinking, and if he's drinking, I don't want to give him any more."

"You never should have offered him the first can of beer," Richard said. "After all, he's supposed to be working for you, not paying a call. You only gave it to him because he's a Negro."

"I was trying to be nice to him," I said.

Richard shrugged impatiently. "And get a little free credit for high principles," he said.

We talked half-heartedly that night of firing Jesse, but there was no one else in town to teach Ralph, and we were not spending enough money on the lessons to care much one way or the other. So we went on with them for almost a year and a half, until we found a white teacher, a high school senior who agreed to take Ralph on. Ralph learned more from that boy in a month than he had learned from Jesse in a year and a half.

About a month before we found the high-school boy to teach Ralph, Jesse told me the story of his childhood. I was driving him home one hot Thursday afternoon in September, when the subject of where he had lived as a child drifted into the conversation. I don't know why we had never talked of his home before. I suppose I had been more interested in his adult life than in his childhood; and I had assumed, too, that he had been born either in or near Philippi, since it had been his headquarters for so long. But for some reason he mentioned Buchanan County that afternoon, and when I asked him if he had ever lived there, he said, yes, he had been born and raised in Buchanan County, ten miles from Pollock, the county seat.

"You live there any after you were grown?" I asked idly.

"No'm," he said. "I left."

"They say it's rough country over there in the hills," I said. "My father told me one time about a feud they had going when he was a boy, just like the Hatfields and McCoys, and they had to call out the National Guard to make them quit killing each other. Did you ever hear about that?"

"Yes ma'am," he said. "I didn't live there at the time. I'd been gone from Buchanan County since I was thirteen. But I heard about it from some of my cousins down to Natchez. It didn't surprise me none. Them white folks been shooting each other for thirty years before they called out the Guard. I remember one night when I was a little bitty boy, they had a fight on the road going past the place where we lived. The white man owned the place and my step-daddy was out looking for a mare had got loose, and the white man got hit in the arm by a stray bullet."

"No wonder you left," I said. I was still trying to keep the conversation going.

Jesse did not answer and, when I glanced at him, he seemed to be deep in thought. His long arm, bent at the elbow, was half out the open window of the car. His shabby old hat was on his lap, and in his left hand he was absently rolling a dead cigarette back and forth. He never smoked in the car with me, and if he got into the car with a lighted cigarette, he always carefully put it out and either put it in his pocket or held it in his hand until he got out. He was perfectly sober that afternoon, dressed in his neat dark suit, his long face the picture of quiet dignity.

We drove on for a block, and stopped at the first of several traffic lights on the way to Jesse's house, before he spoke again. Then he repeated himself. "Born and raised in Buchanan County," he said. "Away out in the country from Pollock. I ain't been back there since I left. Thirteen years old when I left, and I been on my own ever since."

"That was pretty young to go on your own," I said.

"I had five brothers and three sisters, and I reckon they all dead but me."

"You must have been the baby, then," I said.

"No ma'am. I had a baby sister," he said. "Died in my arms. So little I didn't know the difference."

I wasn't sure what he meant, although at first I thought he was saying that she was so small, so frail, he couldn't tell when the life went out of her. And I assumed that he was talking about some time recently, that his sister had been an old woman when she died.

"What?" I said. I always hopefully asked him to repeat himself when our conversations got confusing, although sometimes the repetition only made them more confusing.

"I was ten years old at the time," he said. "And she was two. I was so little I didn't know she was dead."

"Oh, *Jesse*," I said. "Where was your mama?"

"My mama was dead," he said. "She been dead six months when the baby died. And so we had nobody but each other. I and her was the two youngest children, and the baby, she was a half to me. Like I told you, I had a step-daddy. *Gret*, big, black nigger; eyes like coals, *hot*; tall, big as a mountain he seemed like to me. I wasn't nothing but a skinny piece of nothing." He smiled and looked down at his thin arm. "I always been skinny," he said. "Food don't put no weight on me."

"But where was he?" I asked. "Who was taking care of you all?"

"*I* taken care of *her*," Jesse said. He nodded his head, as if even now he could say that he was satisfied with the way he had cared for his little sister. "Ain't it hot?" he said.

We had turned now, down a dusty side street between rows of shotgun houses set on twenty-foot lots. I slowed down to let half a dozen little Negro boys, who were playing ball in the street, get out of the way. We raised a cloud of choking dust as we drove, even going so slowly, and it settled on dusty shrubs and porches, and in a gray film on the children's dark, sweat-streaked bodies.

"I loved that little baby," Jesse said. "She was the prettiest thing you ever seen. She was light like my mama. I takes my dark color from my daddy. She would follow me around and mind me good as if I was a man; and I had to be mama and daddy both to her, if I was but ten. I always loved children ever since, because she was took from me, I reckon, and I been sorry I had none of my own."

"But where was your step-daddy?" I said. "Weren't there any grown people around?"

"Well," he said, "us two lived together in a cabin on a place belonged to some white people over there in Buchanan County. My step-daddy was no good. Soon as my mama died he went off to work in the next county. Left us. And I was just as glad, I was so scared of him. He had a terrible hot rage on him. Most times I could run, but he would of kilt that baby sooner or later. He would come around maybe once in a month to see how we was getting along, and that was too soon to suit me. If I never saw him, it would of been too much. And, like I told you, my other brothers and sisters was all older than me, grown by the time my mama died—twelve years old or more, and all but two out taking care of themselves. Them two left when she died. Oh, Lord, they was scattered over the country. Some I don't ever remember seeing in my life. And yet, my mama wasn't so old when she died. She had her first when she was fifteen, so my uncle told me, once. I had this uncle, see, my mama's brother, Will Hobson was his name, lived down the road from us about five miles, and he used to come around regular every week to see how we was doing. He would cut us a stack of wood when we needed it. But he had plenty children of his own, ten or twelve, and a mean wife. He would of took us in, but she wouldn't have us." He hesitated and then corrected himself. "I don't blame her. I did wrong to say she was mean. She had more than she could feed already. And like I say, he come around regular to see after us. The white people where we stayed was good to us, too. They could just as easy have took the house from us after my mama died and my step went off, but they didn't. I used to go up to their house every so often and they'd give me a sack of meal, and meat, and molasses. I could cook pretty good. They give us blankets, too, because my step, he took all the covers when he went. And the white man come down and turned a garden for me to plant greens and such that spring, but after all we didn't stay long enough to eat them. I fished, too. I will say for myself, I could catch plenty fish even then."

He paused, and I said nothing, already so heartsick at the story he was telling me that I wanted to hear no more of it. But he went on after a minute.

"I didn't have no sense," he said. "I wasn't nothing but a kid." He waved his arm at a cluster of children standing on a street corner, quarreling in loud voices. "No older than the biggest of them. And so I reckon the baby, she was sick two, three days, probably, without me knowing it. She probably had a fever or something. Anyways, I remember she cried a lot, and I would put her in the bed and get in with her to try and quiet her down. I got *so* tired hearing her cry. And at night we would sleep together. One Saturday night we was laying together in the bed, me holding her and patting her. She'd been crying and crying 'most all day, until I was so mad and tired I didn't think I could listen to her no more. I was ready to go off and leave her. And all of a sudden she quit. She just went to sleep. And I was glad. I was so tired I slept, too, after she quit crying, all that night and most of the next morning. When I finally got up, I tippied out in the kitchen to fix us some breakfast without bothering her. But it was ready and still she didn't wake. I ate and I didn't even go back in to her. Lord, I needed a little peace. She slept and she slept. But I didn't think nothing of it one way or the other. Least I can't remember I did. I reckon I was still glad she was sleeping and not crying. So I let her be all that day. And that evening, long about dusk-dark, my uncle, the one lived down the road, come along and I was out in the yard playing. I remember it all like it was yesterday. He was not much taller than you, Miss, and thin. You wouldn't think he could of had all them children, much less taken care of them. But he was *strong*. He could chop *wood*. I never seen a man could handle a ax no better than him. And he could pick three hundred pounds of cotton every day. I wished sometimes it would of been so he could take me and my sister in that year. We wouldn't of been no trouble to him, not if I could help it. Anyway, he come along the road there by the house and stopped, and I was sitting under a big old chinaberry tree in the front yard, just sitting, playing some game or other to myself, I reckon, but I don't remember what.

"'How you all getting along, Jess?' he says.

"'Fine,' I say. 'We getting along just fine.'

"'You need me to cut you some wood this week?' he says.

"'No sir,' I say. 'We got plenty, Uncle Will.'

"He squats down there in the dust by me under the chinaberry tree, like he does 'most every week when he comes by, to talk awhile.

"'What you been doing all day long, son?' he says.

"'Just playing,' I say.

"'How your garden coming along?'

"'Greens is up. We ought to get a good mess by the end of the week.'

"He looks all around the yard. 'Where the baby?' he says.

"'She in the house,' I say. 'She sleep.'

"'Taking a nap, huh?' he says.

"'Yes sir, she been taking a nap all day.'

"'*What you say, boy?*'

"'She been sleep all day,' I say, 'and last night, too. She ain't cried once.'

"Course by that, he knew something was wrong. 'Come on,' he says. 'We better go wake her up.'

"So we went in the house and she was laying up in the bed all under the covers as quiet, and I watched him, and he turned back the covers and felt her and she was cold. Dead." Jesse nodded his head. "I reckon she been dead all day," he said, "and all the night before, ever since she stopped crying. But I never knew it. We took and buried her that afternoon, my uncle and me."

I was so sick I couldn't say anything except, "Oh, *Jesse.*"

We had reached Jesse's neat little house on Pearl Street now, and I drew up to the curb and stopped. But he did not get out of the car. Instead he went on with his story matter of factly.

"My mama was third wife to my step," he said. "My own daddy died when I was no more than two or three. I can't remember him. Like I said, I was eighth child to him. And he was a settled man when my mama married him. She didn't marry again for a long time after he died. She went back and stayed with her own daddy until *he* died. And then she married my step. She was sorry afterwards; she left him two, three times, took me and what other kids was with her and tried to make it on her own, but she couldn't. You know, Miss, nobody going to give no lone woman with children no crop to make. How could she do it? And so she would have to go back to him."

He paused and looked at me as if waiting for my comment, but I could not speak. I gripped the steering wheel with both hands and stared at him, concentrating on keeping the tears from coming to my eyes. He went on quietly.

"She always done the best she could for us," he said. "Hard

times or good, she seen we went to school. All but two of us, my uncle told me, finished the sixth grade. And me, of course, because she died when I was in the fifth. But I could already write a good hand. It come easy to me. And she could cook, too, and sew, better than most. It never seemed right to me how bad my step done her, and she a good woman. I heard when I was grown that he beat the first two wives he had to death. And my mama, you wouldn't know it from looking at a great, skinny old man like me, but she was a little bitty mite of a thing, like a bird, a little brown pecky bird. He killed her, too. Might not of struck the blow that did it, but he *killed* her. Wore her and beat her to death. I seen him more than once take her by the heels and throw her through the door."

"Oh, Jesse," I said. "Where were the police and the sheriff? Couldn't somebody do something about him?"

"Miss, nobody cared about things like that in them days," Jesse said.

"I don't see how a little boy could live through such times and not be crazy," I said.

"I run off from there when I was thirteen," he said. "For a while after my little sister died, I stayed with a old man down the road didn't have no children and needed somebody to help him around his place. Then that winter my step come back. Lost the crop he'd had in the next county and they wouldn't keep him on. He didn't have nobody to help him and couldn't make it on his own, so he come back and got me. He kept me two years and I had no place to turn. He beat me some, but I was getting a big boy. Not big enough to beat *him*, but big enough to outrun him if I got a start, and big enough to know I would be big enough to beat him soon. So one day, when I was thirteen, he caught me. He like to kilt me before I got loose from him, whaling me with the buckle end of his belt. I tore my shirt half off and run out in the road by our house and stood there in the dirt crying and screaming like a baby. 'I'll kill you,' I screamed. 'I'll kill you. I'll kill you.' And he stood on the porch sweating and catching his breath, and laughed at me. But I would have. I left that day, and I never went looking for him, but if I'd ever of seen him again, I would of killed him. I still would. But he's dead now, bound to be."

Jesse put on his hat, opened the car door, and got out. He opened the back door and, reaching in, pulled out his battered guitar case. "Man, it's hot today," he said again. When he had closed the back door he bent down to the front window and took off his hat. "You see, Miss," he said, gesturing behind him toward the washtub by his front steps, "them petunias and merrygolds bloomed out, but my wife got chrysanthemums coming on now in the back. I'm going to bring you a bunch when they begin to bloom."

"That'll be nice," I said. "Thank you."

"Well," he said, "I'll be seeing you Monday. I thank you for the ride." He straightened up and put on his hat again. "May you and the cap'n have a pleasant weekend," he said.

Jesse worked for us only about a month after that day. He came to the next two lessons drunk, and Richard and I made up our minds that we had to find someone else to teach Ralph. We didn't tell Jesse why. I just said that I thought Ralph was too young, that he had learned as much as he could at his age, and we thought he should drop the lessons until he was older. Jesse agreed.

"He ain't made much progress lately," he said. "He ain't got his mind on it."

I haven't seen the old man since, except at a distance. I heard that he had bought an old car, and then shortly afterwards that he had been arrested for drunk driving. He didn't call on us to bail him out.

But a strange thing happened recently. I woke up one night from a nightmare about Jesse. I couldn't remember anything about it except that it had been long and confused, with a great many people in it, and Jesse wandering in and out, a child no older than Ralph, but skinny instead of stocky as Ralph is, and having not a child's head on his shoulders, but the long, seamed face and high, domed forehead of his old age. I was choking with anxiety when I woke up, and two sentences kept repeating themselves over and over in my mind until, to exorcise them and sleep again, I turned on the light and wrote them in the margin of a magazine on my night table. When I got up the next morning, I could not remember what I had written or why, in the night, it had seemed so important. I picked up the magazine and read, "There are those of us who are willing to say, 'I am guilty,' but who is to absolve us? And do we expect by our confessions miraculously to relieve the suffering of the innocent?" I had written first, "Do we expect to *escape* the suffering of the innocent?" but I had scratched through *escape* and written *relieve*. I read the sentences over several times, but they did not dispel the anxiety I still felt. I remembered then the reason I had written them. I had thought in the night that if I could remember those words, I would understand everything. But the words were only questions. It wouldn't have mattered if I had forgotten them.

I Just Love Carrie Lee

(Homochitto)

ALL THE TIME we were away from here, living in Atlanta, I paid Carrie Lee's wages—seven dollars a week for eight years. Of course, part of the time, after Billy married and came back to Homochitto, she was working for him in the country. She rides the bus to Wildwood, seven miles over the river, every day. I don't know why she doesn't move back over there, but she likes to live in town. She owns her own house and she likes to visit around. The truth of the matter is, she thinks she might miss something if she moved over the river; and besides, she never has had any use for "field niggers." (That's Carrie Lee talking, not me.) Anyway, as I was saying, I did pay her wages all those years we were away from here. I knew Mama would have wanted me to, and besides, I feel the same responsibility towards her that Mama did. You understand that, don't you? She was our responsibility. So few people think that way nowadays. Nobody has the feeling for Negroes they used to have. People look at me as if they think I'm crazy when I say I paid Carrie Lee all that time.

I remember when I first had an inkling how things were changing. It was during the Depression when the Edwardses moved next door to us. They were Chicago people, and they'd never had any dealings with Negroes. Old Mrs. Edwards expected the baseboards to be scrubbed every week. I suppose she scrubbed them herself in Chicago. Oh, I don't mean there was anything wrong with her. She was a good hard-working Christian soul; and *he* was a cut above *her*. I've heard he came from an old St. Louis family. But a woman sets the tone of a household, and her tone was middle-western to the marrow. All her children said "come" for "came" and "I want in," and I had a time keeping mine from picking it up.

To make a long story short, she came to me one day in the late fall and asked me what the yardmen in Homochitto did in the winter.

"What do you mean?" I said.

"I mean where do they work?"

"Well," I said, "mine sits around the kitchen and shells pecans and polishes silver all winter."

"You mean you keep him on when there's actually nothing for him to do?" she said.

"He *works* for us," I said. "He's been working for us for years."

"I haven't got that kind of money," she said. "I had to let mine go yesterday, and I was wondering where he would get a job."

I tried to explain to her how things were down here, how you couldn't let a man go in the winter, but she didn't understand. She got huffy as could be.

"I suppose that's what you call *noblesse oblige,*" she said.

"You could, if you wanted to be fancy," I said.

And do you know what she said to me? She said, "They're not going to catch me in that trap, the *Nee*-grows. I can do all my own work and like it, if it comes to that. I'm going to stand on my rights."

They didn't stay in Homochitto long.

Wasn't that odd? Everyone is like that nowadays. Maybe not for such a queer reason, but no one feels any responsibility any more. No one cares, white or black.

That's the reason Carrie Lee is so precious to us. She cares about us. She knows from experience what kind of people we are. It's a boon in this day and age just to be recognized.

The truth of the matter is I couldn't tell you what Carrie Lee has meant to us. She's been like a member of the family for almost fifty years. She raised me and she's raised my children. Ask Sarah and Billy, Carrie Lee was more of a mother to them than I was. I was too young when I first married to be saddled with children, and too full of life to stay at home with them. Bill was always on the go, and I wouldn't have let him go without me for anything. It was fortunate I could leave the children with Carrie Lee and never have a moment's worry. She loved them like they were her own, and she could control them without ever laying a hand on them. She has her own philosophy, and while *I* don't always understand it, children do.

Carrie Lee is a bright Negro—both ways, I mean, and both for the same reason, I reckon. I don't know exactly where the white blood came from (it's not the kind of thing they told young ladies in my day), but I can guess. Probably an overseer. Her mama was lighter than she, and married a dark man. The old mammy, Carrie Lee's grandmother, was black as the ace of spades, so Mama said. I judge some overseer on Grandfather's place must have been Carrie Lee's grandfather. She has always said she has Indian blood, too, said her mama told her so. But how much truth there is in that I don't know. The hawk nose and high cheekbones look Indian, all right, and there is something about her—maybe that she won't make a fool of herself to entertain you. You know she's different. And she could put the fear of God into the children, like a Cherokee chief out after their scalps.

Billy says Carrie Lee taught him his first lesson in getting along with people. He was the youngest boy in the neighborhood, and of course the other children made him run all their errands; they teased and bullied him unmercifully until he was big enough to stand up for himself. This is the kind of thing they'd do. One day in the middle of my mah-jongg club meeting, he came running in the house crying. Some of the children had mixed up a mess of coffee grounds and blackberry jam and tried to make him eat it. It was an initiation. They formed a new club every week or two and Billy was the one they always initiated.

"Mama's busy, honey," I said. "Tell it to Carrie Lee. She'll tend to 'em for you."

Carrie Lee took him on her lap like a baby and rocked him and loved him until he stopped crying, and then he sat up and said, "But Carrie Lee, who am I going to play with? Everybody's in the club but me."

And she said, "Honey, they bigger than you. If you wants to play, you gits on out there and eats they pudding. If you don't like it, you holds it in your mouth and spits it out when they ain't looking."

"But s'pose they feed me more than I can hold in my mouth?" he said.

"Honey, if they does, you got to make your mouth stretch," she said.

Billy has never forgotten that.

Carrie Lee came to work for Mama when she was fourteen years old. She was only a child, it's true, but even then she had more sense than most grown Negroes. Mama had seen her on their place outside Atlanta and taken a fancy to her. *Her* mother (Carrie Lee's, I mean) cooked for the manager's family there, and Carrie Lee was already taking care of five or six younger brothers and sisters while the mother was at work. You can imagine what it meant to her to come to town. Mama clothed her and fed her and made a finished servant of her. Why, she even saw to it that Carrie Lee went to school through the fifth grade; she'd never been able to go more than a couple of terms in the country. Fifty years ago, practically none of the Negroes went more than a year or two, if that long. When they were seven or eight, they either went to the field or stayed at home to nurse the younger ones.

By the time we moved to Homochitto, Mama couldn't have gotten along without Carrie Lee, and so she came with us. At first Mama was miserable here—homesick for Georgia and her own family and the social life of Atlanta. Compared to Atlanta, Homochitto then was nothing but a village. And the weather! We had never been through a Mississippi summer before, or, for that matter, a Georgia summer; we'd always gone to the mountains—Monteagle, or White Sulphur Springs, or some place like that. But that first year in Homochitto Papa couldn't leave, and Mama got in one of her stubborn spells and wouldn't go without him. To tell you the truth, I think she wanted him to see her suffer, so he'd take her back to Atlanta. She used to say then that no one understood how she felt except Carrie Lee. And I suppose it's true that Carrie Lee missed her family too, in spite of the hard life she'd had with them. In the mornings she and Mama would sit in the kitchen peeling figs or pears or peaches, or washing berries, preserving together, and Carrie Lee would tell stories to entertain Mama. I'd hang around and listen. I remember one day Carrie Lee had said something 'specially outrageous, and Mama said, "Carrie Lee, I don't believe half you say. Why do you make up those awful tales?"

Carrie Lee stopped peeling pears and began to eat the peelings. She always did eat the peelings when they were preserving, everything except figs—a hangover from hungry days, I reckon. She hushed talking a minute, eating and thinking, and then she looked at Mama and said:

"To keep us from the lonely hours,
And being sad so far from home."

It was just like a poem. I had to get up and run out of the house to keep them from seeing me cry. Do you suppose she understood what she'd said and how beautifully she'd said it? Or is it something about language that comes to them as naturally as sleeping—and music?

When Mama died, I felt as if she had more or less left Carrie Lee to me, and I've been taking care of her ever since. Oh, she's no burden. There's no telling *how* much money she has in the bank. There she is, drawing wages from Billy and from me, owns her own house and rents out a room, nobody to spend it on but herself and one step-daughter, and she never has to spend a dime on herself. Between us, Sarah and I give her everything she wears; and as for her house, every stick she has came out of our old house.

When we sold the house, after Mama died, Carrie Lee took her pick of what was left. Of course, I had gotten all the good pieces—the things that were bought before the war—but she wouldn't have wanted them anyway; nothing I chose would have suited her taste. She has a genius for the hideous. She took the wicker porch chairs—you know, the kind with fan backs and magazine racks in the arms and trays hooked onto the sides for glasses—and painted them blue and put them in her living room; and she took a set of crocheted table mats that Mama made years ago. (They were beautiful things, but if you've ever had a set, you know what a nuisance they are. Not a washwoman in Homochitto does fine laundering any more, and *I* certainly wouldn't wash and starch and stretch them *myself*. And besides, where would anyone in a small apartment like this keep those devilish boards with nails in them, that you have to stretch them on?) Anyway, Carrie Lee took those place mats and put them on the wicker chairs like antimacassars, if you can believe it. But that's just the beginning. All the junk collected by a houseful of pack rats like Bill's family—the monstrosities they acquired between 1890 and 1930 would be something to read about. And Bill and Mama had stored everything in Mama's attic when Bill sold his father's house in 1933. Why, I couldn't say, except that Bill always hated to throw anything away. That's a trait that runs in his family: they hang on to what they have. And if his father hadn't hung on to Wildwood during hard times and good, where would we be now?

Fortunately, he did hang on to it, and to everything else *his* father left him. You know, Bill's family didn't have the hard time most people had after the Civil War. His grandfather started the little railroad line from Homochitto to Jackson that was eventually bought by the Southern. He was a practical businessman and he didn't sit back like so many people, after we were defeated, and let his property get away from him out of sheer outrage. And so, the family was able to travel and to buy whatever was stylish at the time. Carrie Lee loved everything they bought, and she has as much of it as she can squeeze into her house: heavy golden oak sideboard and table, a fine brass bed polished up fit to blind you, a player piano that doesn't work, with a Spanish shawl draped over it, and on the walls souvenir plates from Niagara Falls and the St. Louis Exposition, and pictures of Mama and me and the children, sandwiched in between pictures of all her sisters and brothers and their families. It's too fine.

Actually, there are some people around here who disapprove of Carrie Lee and me; but as far as I'm concerned they can say what they like. I just love Carrie Lee and that's all there is to it. When she comes to call, she sits in the parlor with the white folks. She has good sense about it. If she's in the house on Sunday afternoon visit-

ing with me, and guests come, she goes to the door and lets them in as if she were working that day, and then she goes back to the kitchen and fixes coffee and finds an apron and serves us. Everything goes smoothly. She knows how to make things comfortable for everybody. But half the time, whoever it is, I wish they hadn't come. I'd rather visit with Carrie Lee.

And people who talk about it don't know what they're saying. They don't know how I feel. When Bill died (that was only a year after Mama died, and there I was, left alone with a houseful of *babies* to raise and all that property to manage), who do you think walked down the aisle with me and sat with me at the funeral? Carrie Lee. If I hadn't been half crazy with grief, I suppose I might have thought twice before I did a thing like that. But I did it, and I wouldn't have let anyone prevent me.

Weddings are a different matter, of course. If you have them at home, it's no problem; the colored folks are all in the kitchen anyhow, and it's easy enough for them to slip in and see the ceremony. I know Winston and Jimmy and the ones we've known for years who turn up at weddings and big parties would *rather* stay in the kitchen. Jimmy takes charge of the punch bowl and sees that all the help stay sober enough to serve, at least until the rector goes home.

But it's not customary in Homochitto to include the servants at a church wedding. There's no balcony in the Episcopal church like the slave gallery in the Presbyterian church, and so there's no place to seat them. I couldn't do anything about that at Sarah's wedding; I just had to leave the rest of the servants out, but we did take Carrie Lee to the church.

I'll never forget how she behaved; if she'd been the mama, she couldn't have been more upset.

Sarah was only nineteen, too young, way too young to marry. To tell you the truth I was crushed at the time. I never, *never* thought any good would come of it. Oh, I realize I was even younger when I married. But in my day young ladies were brought up for marriage, and marriages were made on other terms, terms I understood. Bill was nearly thirty when we married, and he had exactly the same ideas Papa had. He simply finished my education. Which proves my contention—that a woman is old enough to marry when she has sense enough to pick the right man. If she doesn't, she isn't ready. That's the way it was with Sarah.

Wesley was just a boy—a selfish, unpredictable boy. He never understood how sheltered Sarah had been, how little she knew of the world, how indulgent we had been with her as a child, how totally unprepared she was for—for him. And afterwards she said it was all my fault. That's children for you. But I hadn't meant to prepare her for *Wesley*. I wouldn't have had him!

To go back to the wedding, Carrie Lee rode to the church with Sarah, and put the finishing touches on her hair and arranged her train. I didn't see this because of course I was sitting in the front of the church, but the people in the back said when Sarah and Brother George started down the aisle, Carrie Lee ran after them, straightening Sarah's train, the tears streaming down her face. I believe she would have followed them to the altar, but Edwin Ware slipped out of his pew and got her to go back. She was crying like a child, saying, "My baby. She's *my baby*."

You'd never have known she had children of her own the way she worshiped mine—still does.

But she had a married interlude. She was too old to carry a child; she had two miscarriages and lost one shortly after it was born. But she raised two or three of her husband's children. Negroes are so funny. Even Carrie Lee, as well as I know her, surprises me sometimes. She turned up at work one morning just as usual. (She never came until ten-thirty, and then stayed to serve supper and wash the dishes at night.) Bertie, who was cooking for me then, had been muttering and snickering to herself in the kitchen all morning, and, when I came in to plan dinner, she acted like she had a cricket down her bosom.

"What in the world are you giggling and wiggling about, Bertie?" I said.

Bertie *fell* out.

Carrie Lee, forty if she was a day, stood there glowering. "You know Bertie, Miss Emma," she said. "Bertie's crazy as a road lizard."

Bertie pointed her finger at Carrie Lee and then she sort of hollered out. "She *ma'ied,* Miss Emma! She ma'ied."

You could have knocked me over with a feather. I didn't even know she was thinking about it. "Are you really, Carrie Lee?" I said.

"Yes'm."

"Well, Carrie Lee!" I said. "My feelings are hurt. Why didn't you tell us ahead of time. We could have had a fine wedding—something special."

I *was* disappointed, too. I've always wanted to put on a colored wedding, and *there,* I'd missed my chance.

Carrie Lee didn't say a word. I never *have* been able to figure out why she didn't tell us beforehand.

And then that nitwit, Bertie, began to laugh and holler again. "She don't need no special wedding, Miss Emma," Bertie said. "Ain't nothing special about getting ma'ied to Carrie Lee."

I was tickled at that, but I was surprised, too. Oh, I'm not so stupid that I don't understand how different Negro morals are from ours. Most of them simply don't have any. And I understand that it all comes from the way things were in slavery times. But our family was different. Grandmother told me many a time that they always went to a lot of trouble with the slave weddings and, after the war, with the tenants'. She kept a wedding dress and veil for the girls to wear, and she made sure everything was done right—license, preacher, reception, and all the trimmings. There was no jumping the broomstick in our family. And Carrie Lee's people had been on our place for generations. I never would have thought she'd carry on with a man.

She seemed devoted to her husband. If she had carried on with one, she must have carried on with others, but I reckon she'd had her fling and was ready to retire. The husband, Henry, was a "settled man," as they say, fifteen years older than Carrie Lee, and had a half-grown son and daughter and two or three younger children. He farmed about thirty acres of Wildwood. I had known the family ever since we moved to Homochitto. (Can you imagine that—my own place, and I didn't know about him and Carrie Lee!)

Later on, shortly before he died, he managed with Carrie Lee's help to buy a little place of his own.

I always let Carrie Lee off at noon on Saturday and gave her all day Sunday, although I hated running after the children. When they got old enough to amuse themselves, it wasn't so bad, but when they were little . . . ! Usually I got Bertie to take over for me. But I never believed in working a servant seven days a week, even when everybody did it, when they were lucky to get Emancipation Day and the Fourth of July. I never treated a servant like that. Bertie had her day off, too.

Henry would be waiting for Carrie Lee in his buggy when she got off on Saturday, and they'd catch the ferry across the river and drive out to Wildwood; and early Monday morning he'd send his son to drive her in to town—it was a couple of hours ride in the buggy. She didn't want to sell her house and move to the country (thank God!) and Henry wouldn't move to town. As Carrie Lee said, he didn't know nothing but farming, and he wasn't fixing to change his ways.

Once in a while she'd take the children to the country with her on Saturday afternoon, and I'd drive over after supper to get them. Every Saturday they begged to go; it was the greatest treat in the world to them to ride to Wildwood in the buggy, and they were crazy about the old man. For a while I kept their horses there, and when Billy was older he used to go over there to hunt. Henry taught him everything he knows about hunting. That was before cotton-dusting killed all the quail in this part of the country.

Well, Carrie Lee lived like that until we moved back to Atlanta, riding to the country every Saturday afternoon and coming in at daybreak on Monday morning. It's hard to understand how anyone could be satisifed with such a life, but Carrie Lee has a happy nature, and of course the fact that she was so much better off financially than most Negroes made a difference. Besides, I wouldn't be surprised if she wasn't glad to have the peace and quiet of a single life during the week. You might say she had her cake and ate it too.

Then I left Homochitto for several years. It's the only time Carrie Lee and I have ever been separated for more than a month or two.

I'd always heard Mama talk about Atlanta; she kept after Papa to go back, right up to his dying day. I'd been too young when we moved to care, but later, after Mama and Bill died, I got the notion that someday I'd go back. So finally, I went. The children were away at school, Billy at Episcopal High and Sarah at Ardsley Hall, and there was no reason for me to stay in Homochitto.

I thought of course Carrie Lee would go with me, but she didn't. For all her talk in Mama's day about how she missed Georgia, she didn't go back. She stayed with Henry. And, as I told you, I paid her wages all the time I was gone. We wrote to each other, and we saw each other when I brought the children to Homochitto for a visit. They never got used to Atlanta and never wanted to stay there in the summer. Then Billy settled in Homochitto and began to farm Wildwood himself, and I came home.

I wish I had kept some of Carrie Lee's letters. She has a beautiful hand. She used to practice copying Mama's script, and finally got so you could hardly tell them apart. It always gives me a turn to get a letter from her, addressed in Mama's hand, and then, inside, what a difference! When she writes something she thinks will amuse me, she puts "smile" after it in parentheses. Did you know that practically all Negroes do that, even the educated ones? I sometimes see pictures of all the ones that are so much in the news nowadays—diplomats and martyrs and so forth, and I wonder if they put (smile) in their letters.

Carrie Lee used to advise me in her letters, where she would never do such a thing face to face. Like one time, I remember, she wrote me, "All the babies is gone, yours and mine. I writes Miss Sarah and Mr. Billy and they don't answer me. True, I got the old man's kids, but you haven't got none. When will you get married again, Miss Emma? Find you a good man to warm your bed." And then she wrote (smile)—to make sure I understood she wasn't being impudent, I reckon.

It was while I was living in Atlanta that Carrie Lee got her picture in the magazine. I never quite understood how it happened, unless through ignorance on all sides—ignorance on the part of the photographer about Carrie Lee's real circumstances, and ignorance on her part about what the photographer wanted. We all laughed about it afterwards, although, of course, I never mentioned it to Carrie Lee.

When we left Homochitto, she had moved over to Wildwood and rented her house in town. That's how they saved enough money for the old man to buy a place of his own. I think she gave him every cent she made. But they had their pictures taken the winter before they bought the place, the last winter they were on Wildwood.

I'll never forget how shocked I was. I had gone out for dinner and bridge one night, and was quietly enjoying a drink when one of the men at the party picked up a copy of *Life* or *Fortune* or one of those magazines.

"By the way," he said to me, "I was reading about your old stamping ground today."

I might have known he was teasing me. None of those magazines ever has anything good to say about Mississippi. But I was interested in news of Homochitto, and never thought of that; and of course *he* didn't know it was Carrie Lee. I sat there while he found the article, and there she was—there they all were, Carrie Lee, Henry, and all the children, staring at me practically life-sized from a full-page picture.

The article was on sharecropping, and *they* were the examples of the downtrodden sharecropper. I must admit they looked seedy. I recognized my dress on Carrie Lee and one of Sarah's on the little girl. They were standing in a row outside the old man's house, grinning as if they knew what it was all about. At least, all of them except Carrie Lee were grinning. She's not much of a grinner.

A November day in the South—the trees bare and black, the stubble still standing in the cotton fields, an unpainted Negro cabin with the porch roof sagging, half a dozen dirty, ragged Negro children, and a bedraggled hound. What more could a Northern editor have asked?

What will these children get for Christmas?

I could have told him what they'd get for Christmas, and who had bought the presents and sent them off just the day before. And I could have told him whose money was accumulating in the teapot on the mantelpiece.

To do them justice, I'll say I don't believe Carrie Lee or Henry had the faintest idea why he'd taken their pictures. They just liked to have their pictures taken. But the very idea of them as poverty-stricken, downtrodden tenants! I couldn't have run them off Wildwood with a posse and a pack of bloodhounds.

We got a big kick out of it. I cut the picture out and sent it to Sarah.

The old man died the year after they began to buy their farm, and then Carrie Lee moved to town, and shortly after that I came back to Homochitto for good. Henry, Jr., took over the payments on the farm and lives on it. He's a sullen Negro—not like his father—but he's good to Carrie Lee. In the summer he keeps her supplied with fresh vegetables; he comes in and makes repairs on her house to save her the price of a carpenter; things like that. But he's sullen. I never have liked these Negroes who're always kowtowing and grinning like idiots—"white folks' niggers," some people down here call them—but it wouldn't hurt that boy to learn some manners. I told Carrie Lee as much one time.

I had gone into the kitchen to see about dinner, and he was sitting at the table with his hat on—this was after we moved back here, and old Henry was dead—eating his breakfast—*my* food, need I add. He didn't even look at me, much less get up.

"Good morning, Henry," I said.

He mumbled something and still didn't get up.

"*Good morning, Henry,*" I said again.

"Morning," he said, just as sullen as he could be.

I went to Carrie Lee later and told her that any man, black, white, blue, or green, could get up and take off his hat when a lady came into the room. That's not prejudice. That's good manners.

"He ain't *bad,* Miss Emma," she said. "Just seems like he always got one misery or another. Born to trouble, as the sparks fly upward, like the Good Book says."

"Well, he'd feel a lot better, if he'd get a smile on that sullen face of his," I said. "Sometimes people bring trouble on themselves just by their dispositions."

"Ah, Miss Emma," she said, "ever since he married, it's been *root, hog, or die* for Henry, Jr. He ain't settled into it yet."

Of course, I didn't know then about the boy's sister, Carrie Lee's stepdaughter. Didn't know she had left Homochitto, much less that she had come back. She apparently married and moved to "*Dee-troit*" while we were living in Atlanta. I didn't see her until some time after she came to live in town with Carrie Lee, just a few years ago. Henry, Jr., finally had to turn her over to Carrie Lee. I can't blame him for *that,* I don't suppose. By then he had five children of his own, and there was scarcely room for them in the house, much less the sister.

I found out about the sister because Sarah left Wesley. That was a hard year. Sarah packed up the children and everything she owned and came home from Cleveland, inconsolable. I suppose I could have said, "I told you so," but I didn't have the heart. She'd married too young, there's no getting around it, and by the time she was old enough to know her own mind, there she was with two children. I tell you, people say to me: "You don't know how lucky you are that Bill left you so well-fixed. Never any money problems." They don't know how wrong they are. Money's a preoccupying worry. It keeps your mind off worse things. If you don't have to work or to worry about money, you're free to worry more about yourself and your children. Believe me, *nobody's* exempt from disappointment. I'm *proud* of the way I've raised my children. I've taught them everything I know about good manners and responsibility and honor, and I've kept their property safe for them. I've tried to give them everything that my family and Bill gave me. But when love fails you, none of it is any use. Your bed is soft and warm, but one dark night you find that sleep won't come.

I was half crazy over Sarah. She slept until noon every day and moped around the house all afternoon. Then she'd start drinking and keep me up till all hours crying and carrying on. "What am I going to do? What am I going to do?"

She still loved that good-for-nothing man.

I borrowed Carrie Lee from Billy to take care of Sarah's babies while she was here. I'm too old to chase a two-year-old child, and Sarah hardly looked at the children. She was too busy grieving over Wesley. So Carrie Lee was a boon; she took over, and we never had a minute's concern for them. Like all children, they adored her.

Billy's wife was furious with me for taking her, but I simply had to. And Carrie Lee was in seventh heaven, back with Sarah and me; she never has gotten along too well with Billy's wife. Oh, she goes out there faithfully, on account of Billy and the children. But Billy's wife is different from us—a different breed of cat, altogether, there's no getting around it. I get along fine with her because I mind my own business, but Carrie Lee considers our business her business. And then too, as I said, Carrie Lee is a *finished* servant. She has run my house for months at a time without a word of direction from me. She can plan and put on a formal dinner for twelve without batting an eye. Billy's wife doesn't know anything about good servants. She tells Carrie Lee every day what she wants done that day; and she insulted her, the first time she had a party, by showing her how to set the table.

No doubt there are two sides to the story. I'm sure Billy's wife gets sick of hearing Carrie Lee say, "But Miss Emma don't do it that way." It must be like having an extra mother-in-law. I won't go into that. I know it's the style nowadays not to get along with your mother-in-law, although I don't see why. I never had a breath of trouble with mine.

But I'm wandering again. I want to tell you the wonderful thing Carrie Lee said when she was telling us about her stepdaughter.

The children were taking their naps one afternoon, and Sarah and I were lying down in my room and Carrie Lee was sitting in there talking to us. Sarah was still thrashing around about Wesley. The truth is she wanted to go back to him. She was hollering to Carrie Lee about how he'd betrayed her and how she could never forgive him—just asking somebody please to find a good reason why she should forgive him, if the truth be known. But I wasn't going to help her; I knew it would never work.

Carrie Lee listened a while and thought about it a while and then she said, "Miss Sarah, honey, you know I got a crazy child?"

That took the wind out of Sarah's sails, and she sat up and stopped crying and said, "What?"

I was surprised, too. I didn't know a thing about that crazy girl. When I thought about it, I remembered that Carrie Lee had mentioned her to me once or twice, but at the time I hadn't paid any attention.

"I got a crazy child," Carrie Lee says. "Least, she ain't exactly my child, she old Henry's. But she *sho* crazy."

"I didn't know that, Carrie Lee," I said. "Where does she stay?"

"She stay with me," Carrie Lee says. "Right there in the house with me. Neighbors tend to her in the daytime. I ain't had her with me long—no more than a year or two."

"Well, what do I care? What's it got to do with me?" Sarah said, and she began to cry again. She wasn't herself, or she wouldn't have been so mean.

"This what," Carrie Lee says, "You know why she crazy? A man driv her crazy, that's why. You don't watch out, a man gonna driv you crazy."

Sarah lay back on the bed and kicked her feet like a baby.

"Honey, you want me to tell you how to keep a man from driving you crazy? And not only a man. Howsomever it happens, the day comes when one of God's creatures, young or old, is bound to break your heart. I'll tell you how to bear it."

Sarah shook her head.

"I'm gonna tell you anyhow. Look at me. I'm sixty years old. I looks forty-five. No man never driv me crazy, nor nobody else. I tell you how I keep him from it."

Sarah couldn't help it. She sat up and listened.

"See everything, see nothing," says Carrie Lee. "Hear everything, hear nothing. Know everything, know nothing. Trust in the Lord and love little children. That's how to ease your heart."

Did you ever? Well sir, maybe Sarah would have gone anyway, or maybe she heeded Carrie Lee's advice. Anyway, she took the two children soon afterwards and went back to Wesley, and it wasn't until three years later that they got a divorce.

So here we are, Carrie Lee and I, getting old. You might say we've spent our lives together. I reckon I know her better than I would have known my own sister, if I had had one. As Carrie Lee would say, "We've seen some wonderful distressing times."

On Sundays, when she's off, lots of times she bakes me a cake and brings it around and we sit and talk of the old days when Mama and Bill were alive and when the children were little. We talk about the days of the flood, about this year's crop, about the rains in April, and in August the dry weather, about Billy's wife, and Sarah and Billy's grown-up troubles, about the grandchildren, and "all the days we've seen."

If she comes to see me on Sunday, Carrie Lee will tell me something that amuses me the whole week long. Like a couple of weeks ago we were talking about the crop. I'd been worrying all summer about the drought. It looked for a while as if Billy wouldn't make a bale to the acre. And every time I mentioned it to Carrie Lee, she'd say, "Trust in the Lord, Miss Emma." She's still a great one for leaving things to the Almighty.

Then, bless John, the cotton popped open, and, in spite of everything, it's a good year.

"Well, Carrie Lee," I said, "it looks like you were right and I was wrong. Billy's got a fine crop."

And Carrie Lee says (just listen to this), she says, "Miss Emma, if I say a chicken dips snuff, you look under his bill."

Isn't that killing? When I got by myself, I just hollered.

Looking at it another way, though, it isn't so funny. Billy's a man, and a son is never the companion to his mother that a daughter is. You know the old saying, "A son is a son till he gets him a wife, but a daughter's a daughter all of her life." I think if his father had lived, if there were a man in the house, Billy would come to see me more often. If Sarah were here, we would enjoy each other, I know; but she's married again and lives so far away, they seldom come home, and when they do, it's only for a few days.

I've never been a reader, either. I like to visit, to *talk*. I'm an articulate person. And nowadays, instead of visiting, people sit and stare at a television set. Oh, I still play cards and mah-jongg. I have friends here, but we drifted apart during the years I was in Atlanta, and things have never been quite the same since I came back.

So I'm often alone on Sunday afternoon when Carrie Lee comes to see me. That's how it happens we sit so long together, drinking coffee and talking. Late in the afternoon, Billy sometimes comes and brings the children to call, but they never stay for long. They go home to Wildwood because Billy's wife doesn't like to be there alone after dark. Carrie Lee stays on, and we go in the kitchen and she fixes my supper. As I've told you, I'd rather visit with her than with most white folks. She understands me. When I think about it, it sometimes seems to me, with Bill and Mama dead and the children grown and gone, that Carrie Lee is all I have left of my own.

Hold On
(Philippi)

Paul and Silas, bound in jail
Had nobody for to go their bail.
Keep your hand on the plow,
Hold on.

They begun to pray and shout.
Walls fell down and they marched right out.
Keep your hand on the plow,
Hold on.

Now, what set Paul and Silas free
Is good enough for you and me.
Keep your hand on the plow,
Hold on.

Oh, the years have come and gone.
Great God, lead us on and on.
Keep your hand on the plow,
Hold on.

Hold on, hold on.
Keep your hand on the plow,
Hold on.

Spiritual

I

IN ANNA GLOVER'S dream, one scene, like a frame from an old movie of which all else has been forgotten, summed up what she had felt that day on the lake: disbelief, terror, helplessness, guilt, and loss. Estella lay face down on the hull of the overturned skiff, and the skiff rocked and sank in the yielding water. For an instant, relief: *she's all right, safe.* Then, kicking, clutching, scrabbling her fingernails along the mossy hull, Estella slid off the other side with a half-strangled grunt, turned on Anna a terrible, glassy stare, and sank.

In the grocery store, at a cocktail party, in the car, waking at night from a sound sleep, Anna did not think of, but *saw* that scene, heard the animal noise of death, felt again her desperate disappointment and helplessness. It was as if sight, touch, sound, turned for the moment inward and retraveled paths grooved nerve end to nerve end in her brain by the memory. For the duration of a heartbeat all the exterior world ceased to impinge, and she was as absorbed, as convinced as in a dream. *It happened*—real as the hallucination of a lunatic.

She would close her eyes and shake herself. The hair would rise on her arms and the muscles of her stomach would contract, her whole body would contract, the very pores closing to shut the horror out. Consciously, if she were alone, she would say to herself, I'll think of something else, and would choose something specific to absorb her attention, whatever was most seductive. Most often she chose an erotic daydream, and would go through an imaginary love affair in her mind to exorcise the dream.

For months it came: no day passed without its return. Later a week would go by without it, so that she relaxed, and then when her mind was open, expecting nothing, she would see it again.

Afterwards she remembered quite clearly the last time the nightmare seized her, and recalled her knowledge, as she shivered and the goose flesh came on her arms, that it was happening for the last time. She was at a concert with her husband. On the brightly-lit stage of the high-school auditorium the members of a woodwind quintet sat and played. The intricate, clear pattern of the Mozart "Quintet for Piano and Woodwinds" laced the air. Light shone from the keys of the long, softly brown bassoon, from the precisely turned ebony of clarinet and oboe, the golden convolutions of the French horn.

The tailcoats of the players dropped in neat black folds on either side of their chairs. But in the darkness of the auditorium Anna heard, not the ageless reassurance that chaos could be brought to heel, but the whoosh and suck of formless depths, the scrape of broken nails against metal, the wind . . . She bent forward, shivering. Her husband Richard, sitting beside her, tall and quiet in his dark suit, his fine aquiline profile immobile and concentrated, felt the shiver against his arm, and turned to her, whispering. "What's the matter? Are you sick?"

She shook her head. "A rabbit ran over my grave."

To herself she said, That's all. That's the last time. Afterwards she could lay her nightmare beside everything else she remembered or had later learned about the accident and examine it all with the same detachment.

She had learned gradually, from one source and another, and from her own ruminations, a great deal, much more than the brief remembered struggle, the hour or moment outside of time which fought for a place in her ordered life. For, during the period when she was suffering the recurrent nightmare, the accident was having another effect on her, one that eventually made it possible to stop dreaming: she *had* to think about it, to talk about it, and to hear about everyone else's part in it.

Everything was pertinent: Gaines Williamson's lacerated hand, her children's silence, the comments of friends and acquaintances, and, most of all, the advent in their lives as a result of the accident of Carl Jensen, who had pulled them out of the water and who became her friend.

Her listening and telling and musing on the story began the day of the accident, in the police car with her husband and the policeman who drove her out to the hospital to be checked over. The two men had half carried, half dragged her up the levee and put her in the car, and as soon as Richard got in beside her, she began to talk.

"She kept pulling me down, she kept pulling me down," she said. "And the water . . . the water . . . I couldn't breathe . . . couldn't keep her up, she was too heavy. I couldn't keep her up."

"Shh, don't talk about it," Richard said. "It's all over. Don't think about it any more. You don't ever have to think about it any more."

"But I want to tell you about it," she said. "I have to tell you about it."

She could not see herself, had no notion of the spectacle she presented—long brown hair pulled loose from its usual neat twist, plastered down on her cheeks and stringing in slimy ropes down her wet back, blouse ripped open from neck to waist, face swollen and distraught. Both men, as she thought afterwards, must have been intent mainly on averting an attack of hysterics. Richard put his arm around her, drew her to him, and patted her on the shoulder. With his other hand he pulled her blouse together across her breasts.

But she did not feel hysterical, or even battered, only that her knees would not hold her up and that she needed a drink. Dimly, too, from the moment when, seeing Estella struggling on the stretcher, she was convinced that she was not dead, from the moment when time began again, she felt that she was—or was she?—a heroine of sorts. She knew that the weakness of her knees was not only physical, but also the appropriate aftermath of such a shattering experience, an impressive external sign of her ordeal. In the same way she knew that the policeman turned on the siren and sped through stoplights on the way to the hospital not because haste was necessary, but out of respect for his own importance. Even then, in the car on the way to the hospital, she could step outside herself to the degree that she recognized, while she yielded to, the need for a certain amount of make-believe.

I'll probably never have a chance to be even a halfway heroine again, she said to herself with a wry, interior laugh.

Anna knew well enough that for her the line between make-believe and reality wavered; that the stories she told herself (even in the middle of the most absorbing act, even about birth and death and making love) sometimes intruded on reality, forcing her to a shocking detachment from her own emotions; that she sometimes thought: I am telling myself a story, and this thought called into question the genuineness of all her feelings. But the story-telling was an inescapable fact, and she had learned to accept it, to shrug off the complicated understanding that for some queer reason she could act, could watch herself act, could create a romance about her actions, and could prick the balloon of her romance all at the same time.

In the police car, siren wailing, lights blinking, Anna clasped her hands together in her lap and, feeling a stab of pain, looked vaguely down and then held her left hand up for Richard to see. It was scraped and bruised across the inside of the fingers and was beginning to swell. "Look," she said "I must have hurt it. I wonder when I did that." And then, "But I want to tell you about what happened."

And so she told him, although, looking into his closed, expressionless face, she knew that what she said caused him too much pain, that he would rather never think or hear anything about it again. Later, after the first flurry and excitement died down, she would not allow herself to mention it to him, not only because the subject made him unhappy, but also because she sensed his disapproval, as if he would like to say: What's the point in talking about it *again?* For Christ's sake, forget it.

But during those first days she talked to everyone: to Richard's father and mother, to her friends, to people who stopped her in the grocery store and asked her about it. And she listened, too, to comments ranging from the grocery clerk's explanation ("Mrs. Glover, I figure you got into a stretch of dead water. Plenty people around here don't know about dead water, but it's a fact, nothing'll float in it. And you can tell it, too. The light don't flash off it even on the sunniest day"), to the contempt of the lawyer acquaintance who stopped her on the street ("That's what you get, Anna, taking a damn nigger out in a boat").

She always told it in the same way, trying to say how everything had happened, not to exaggerate or forget. But in spite of this, it struck her from something Carl Jensen said, when she went to call on him to thank him for saving their lives, that perhaps she was not telling the truth.

"You were in the water there by the boat," Jensen said, "and I said, 'Come on, I'll help you in,' and you said, 'No, get this one first.' I hadn't even realized you had hold of the colored woman. I hadn't seen her. She was underwater. You pulled on her belt and she came up. My God! You were holding her belt and she was floating underwater, out of sight."

Until he said that, Anna had remembered herself as holding Estella by the hair, had remembered the feel of stiff, greasy hair against her fingers. Now she knew that Jensen was right, she had had hold of her belt; and she saw the implication of her mistake. Everything she remembered or thought she remembered about "it" might be wrong. In the dark depths of herself she might be creating another story, a false version of what had happened in the dark depths of the lake. She went home and sought out her son Ralph and questioned him.

"I know you don't like to think about the accident," she told him, "or hear people talk about it." (For he always left the room when it was discussed, and, like his father, seemed forced to put away from himself the feelings that he knew would make him miserable.) Anna paused, watching his expressionless face, then went on. "I have to ask you about it this one more time," she said. "You see, I keep thinking about it, and sometimes I think to myself that it was not the way I remember it at all. Maybe I was so scared I changed it. I want you to tell me once exactly how you think it happened, so I'll know. Steve is too little, and I can't ask Murray, he never answers, and you're the only other one who was there."

And so he told her. She was not sure whether she had prompted him to get out of him some of the details which she recalled so vividly, and she could not avoid recognizing that he might have got his version not from the accident but from hearing her tell it. But at least, she said to herself, he didn't disagree so violently with the way I saw it that he had another verison to give me when I asked for it. With that she had to be satisfied.

It was typical of Carl Jensen, as she later knew, that when she began to look for him no one had ever heard of him. The newspaper account of the accident did not mention him, giving the whole credit for the rescue to Gaines Williamson, the Negro bartender and caretaker at the Yacht Club. Richard had not seen him and the police officers did not know who he was. She located him finally through Gaines, who knew him because he spent most of his free time on the lake and had bought gas and oil for his boat several times at the Yacht Club.

"He ain't been around here long, Mrs. Glover," Gaines said when she telephoned to ask about him. "I know everybody in town that goes out on the lake any, and he *stays* on the lake. He must have moved here long about April, because that's when I first begun seeing him. He come down here the first day he got to town, I bet. But he don't fish. No'm, he don't ski or nothing. Mostly he walks. He walks around the lake once a week anyway. He don't have no boat of his own, but sometimes he rents a boat down to Mr. Ferguson's dock and goes over to the island. That was one of Mr. Ferguson's boats he was in the other day. He's bound to know where you can find him . . . No'm, I don't know his name. Just know I sell him gas once in a while."

Mr. Ferguson told Anna that her rescuer's name was Carl Jensen. "He's an odd fellow, Mrs. Glover," he said. "A loner. I don't know where he lives, but he told me he worked at the radio station."

From the radio station she got his address and found out that he was off for the weekend and that he did not have a telephone. The afternoon of the third day after the accident she went to see him.

He lived in a small apartment in the oldest section of Philippi, three blocks from the levee. The house was old, one of those story-and-a-half gingerbread houses that line the down-at-the-heels side streets of Southern towns, set back from the street under two spreading water oaks. The whole place—house, lot, straggly Phitzer junipers, buckling sidewalk, and sagging gallery—had the look of a moribund boarding house run by an aging slattern. The house number that the radio station had given her was painted above the side door in staggering black letters. The door was open. She looked in.

I really am crazy, she thought. I'm as bad as Estella. I must be having some kind of hallucination.

Inside the door, stretched across it on the floor so that no one could get in, lay the body of a man, face downward, head resting on his arm.

She turned to leave, then changed her mind. He must be asleep, she thought, and I do want to see him. This is silly. She looked again, realized that the man had wavy, dark hair, saw the deep curving line from nostril to chin, so incongruous in his youthful face (he could not have been more than thirty-one or -two), and recognized her rescuer.

"Mr. Jensen?" she said softly. "Are you awake?"

He moaned and stirred and again she started to leave. Maybe he's drunk, she thought. But he sat up, shaking his head and muttering, stared at her for a minute, and then stood up.

"Yes?" he said warily. He had not recognized her.

"Mr. Jensen?" she said again. "I'm Anna Glover."

Still he stared at her, uncomprehending.

"Don't you remember me?" she said. "I'm the one you pulled out of the lake the other day. Anna Glover. And I came by to . . ."

"Mrs. Glover," he said. And then, "I didn't recognize you." He smiled apologetically. "You don't look the same," he said. "Come in."

"Of course," she said. "I had forgotten how terrible I must have looked. My hair . . . and my clothes torn half off. And besides, I waked you out of a sound sleep."

He held the screen door open and she walked in.

"That's all right," he said in a deep, careful voice. "You must have thought I was crazy, lying on the floor like that. But it's the coolest place in the house, the only place where I can get a breath of air. Sit down," he said. "Please. I've been meaning to call and ask how you were."

They sat down in two ancient armchairs with worn upholstery and uneven springs, and looked at each other uneasily. The furniture in the room was drab and old, faded like the walls to the dirty shades of gray and brown, tan and beige that are the color of all cheap furnished apartments. Anna glanced once around the room, and knew that she was not to deal with what she had expected: this was not to be a brief call, formal courtesy on both sides, and no more. She had wondered as she started up the walk how they would get through it, how you talked to someone who had saved your life and then walked away and forgot him; and had thought to herself of some proverb she had read (was it Chinese?) that he who saves a man's life is responsible thenceforward for his soul. Was that how it went? Then she was responsible for Estella's soul, and this strange man for hers. It seemed to be backwards. Now all these thoughts—what to say, how to put him at ease and make him see how grateful she was, whether or not to offer to pay for the life preserver that the Negro soldier had cut off Estella, how to leave gracefully—all these problems left her mind, replaced by the conviction that they were going to be friends. The glance around the walls that revealed this to her had fallen hastily on bookshelves packed with books, on boxes of books stacked on the floor, on some pieces of driftwood piled in a corner, and then on the picture. It was Rousseau's "Sleeping Gypsy." She looked at the vast, empty landscape, the piercing eye of the lion bent on the unconscious man, and then at Jensen.

"I don't know where to begin," she said. "How do you thank somebody for saving your life?" And she told him about the Chinese proverb.

"Yes," he said, "I've read that." He smiled shyly at her. "You've got yourself a poor guardian," he said, "but I'll do the best I can. Would you like a can of beer for starters?"

"That would be fine," she said.

He went to the closet and got two cans out of his little icebox, opened them, and brought her one.

"I didn't really save your life, you know," he said. "I just pulled you out of the lake. You had already done all the work and were holding on to the boat, waiting."

"I'm afraid I couldn't have waited much longer," she said. "I'd given out."

"I don't see how you held on to her at all," he said. And then he told her what a shock it had been when she brought Estella to the surface. "All I could think was: My God, how am I going to get that woman into the boat? She's huge, isn't she? Is she as big as I re-member her?"

Anna nodded. "She's bigger than God, I think. How did you happen to see us, anyhow? Where were you? When the boat sank, I didn't see anyone."

"I'd beached my boat on the island and was sitting there looking at the storm," he said. "I'd planned to take a walk on the island and was trying to make up my mind whether to go on and get drenched or to go back on the dock, when I heard your children screaming. I must have been about a quarter of a mile down the lake and back in a willow thicket. That's why you didn't see me. And I think the only reason I heard you was the wind. A kind of freakish puff of wind brought the children's voices to me as clear as if they were right there." He shivered. "It was queer, Mrs. Glover," he said. "And to tell the truth, I'm a damn coward. You're lucky I made up my mind to come get you instead of taking to the woods like a rabbit."

"You came," she said. "I don't think you need to worry about what you might have done."

"Do you mind talking about it?" he asked. "Would you rather talk about something else?"

She shook her head. "I'm boring everybody to distraction with it," she said. "And the funny thing is that I haven't yet learned how to say what I want to say. I haven't decided what I mean."

"Well, if you don't mind," he said, "tell me how it happened."

L A T E   S U M M E R in Philippi is a deadly time of year. Other parts of the United States are hot, it is true, but not like the lower Mississippi valley. Here the shimmering heat—the thermometer standing day after day in the high nineties and the nights breathless and oppressive—is compounded even in a drought by the saturated air. Thunderheads, piling up miles high in the afternoon sky, dwarf the great jet planes that fly through them, buffeted by updrafts from the fields spread-eagled in torment under the pulsing sun. But no rain falls from the gigantic clouds. Dust devils—small whirlwinds that form in the dry furrows—go careening off across gray-green fields like living demons bent on some terrible work of destruction. The air is heavy with moisture, and the farmers look into the sky and curse, demanding that God give them exactly the right amount of rain: not so much that the weevils will thrive and the cotton rot on the stalk, nor so little that the beans and pastures will be burnt up, but exactly the right amount.

Lake Okatukla begins to fall. The lake, named for a meandering bayou that flows into it on the Arkansas side, bounds the little town of Philippi on the west. An old horseshoe-shaped bend of the Mississippi, it is blocked off from the river at its northern end by the Nine Mile Dyke, built years ago when a cut-through was made to straighten the course of the river. The southern end of the lake is still a channel into the river through which pass towboats pushing strings of barges loaded with gravel, sand, cotton, scrap iron, soybeans, fertilizer, or oil. Shipping is one of Philippi's most prosperous industries, and towboats built and launched at her terminal travel the river from Cairo to New Orleans: the *Sally B.*, the *Gay Rosey Jane,* the *Jessica,* and a dozen more.

In August, as the lake drops steadily lower and the river silts up the channel opening, big dredge barges move up the river from the Engineer's Station at Vicksburg and set to work dredging the bottom of the south end of the lake, spewing out fountains of mud and sand to keep a nine-foot draft clear for shipping. But higher up, close to the town, where the lake is more than a mile wide, the steely surface water hides depths that never have to be dredged. Around the rusty barges that serve as a terminal, and around the old quarter boat tied up at the foot of the levee and converted into the Philippi Yacht Club, mud flats appear overnight, covered with discarded beer cans, broken bottles, and tangles of baling wire. The surface of the mud cracks and scales like the skin of some monstrous, scrofulous beast, and a deathlike stench pervades the hot still air. But fifty feet out from the lowest mud flat, oil slicks rock, opalescent, over the deep water.

Even in this terrible heat, at noon on the hottest day of the year, breathing this foul, fishy air, there will always be a few Negroes fishing off the terminal barges, bringing in a slimy catfish or a half-dead bream from the oily water, raising their long cane poles and casting out their bait over and over again with dreamlike deliberation, while the shouts of Negro children, swimming off the gravel dump a hundred yards downstream, now and then break the silence, and a brown dock hand sullenly snubs a towboat against the terminal, as if he will never lift a rope again.

In town there has been nothing to do for weeks. Merchants doze in empty stores while outside the traffic lights signal stop and go to deserted streets. The affluent have taken their children to the mountains or the beach; the semi-affluent sweat out their afternoons at the municipal swimming pool and their evenings at the drive-in movies; the poor sit on their porches in the evening and watch their children playing kick-the-can on the dusty street or catching huge beetles under the corner streetlights.

Late in August, if rain falls all along the course of the Mississippi, there will be a rise on the lake as the river backs into it. The mud flats are covered. The trees put on pale spikes of new growth. The sandbars are washed clean. Mud runnels stream from the rain-heavy willow fronds and the willows lift their heads. The fish are biting again.

For a week or two, from the crest of the rise, when the still water begins to clear, dropping the mud that the river has poured into the lake, until another drop has exposed the mud flats, Lake Okatukla is beautiful—a serene broad wilderness of green trees and bright water, bounded at the horizon by the green range of levee sweeping in a slow curve against the sky. Looking down into the water one can see through drifting forests of moss the quick flash of frightened bream, the shadowy threat of great saw-toothed gar. Solitary fishermen are out in their skiffs, casting for bass around the trunks of the big willow trees or fishing with cane poles and minnows for white perch along the fringe willows. The lake is big—twelve miles long with dozens of curving inlets and white sandy islands, a mile or more wide at its broadest point; hundreds of fishermen can spend their days trolling its shores and scarcely disturb one another.

It was one day just after the crest of the August rise in 1957 when Anna Glover took two of her own children, Ralph and Steve, and one of Ralph's friends, Murray McCrae, on a fishing trip. The children had been begging for weeks to be taken on a picnic, and she had put them off, hating the thought of the blood-warm water and the stinking mud flats; but now rain had fallen and she was as eager as they for a day on the lake. The waterfront was deserted when they drove over the crest of the levee. Anna parked the car near the water at the foot of the rough, concrete-cobbled slope, and had begun to unload their gear—life jackets for the children, tackle box, bait, poles, gas can, and Scotch cooler full of beer, soft drinks and sandwiches—when she thought she heard someone shouting her name.

"Miss Anna! Hey, Miss Anna!"

She looked around, but seeing the whole slope of the levee empty and no one on the deck of the Yacht Club except Gaines Williamson, she called the children back from the water's edge, and began to distribute the gear among them to carry down to the fishing skiff which the Glovers kept tied up at one of the Yacht Club floats.

At thirty-six Anna looked scarcely old enough to have three strapping sons. The round peasant face of her childhood had been refined by maturity, the cheekbones and chin were more prominent, the chin, particularly, betraying by its jut a disproportionate, self-willed determination; but her high, rounded brow and brown eyes were clear. There were no lines, either of weariness or of pain, only the two deep vertical marks between her brows that came from the concentrated frown of near-sightedness, and about her wide mouth the faintly sorrowful look of her mother's family that resulted from a slight blurring of the bow of the upper lip. Her long hair, once sandy blond, had darkened to sandy brown; she wore it drawn to a twist on the back of her head. She had a strong, boyish figure, narrow-hipped and flat across the buttocks, and now she heaved the heavy cooler out of the car without much effort and untied the poles from the rack on the side of the car, talking as she worked.

"Ralph, you and Murray carry the cooler; Steve can take the poles. I believe it's going to take two trips to get everything down. Here, boys, wake up and lend a hand."

They gathered around her. Ralph, at ten, was stout and sturdy; his straight nose, solemn expression, and erect sway-backed carriage made him look like a small preacher. Steve, two years younger, had brown eyes like his father's, fringed with a breathtaking sweep of dark lashes, and his mother's mouth. They were beautiful children, or so Anna thought, for she regarded them with the most intense and subjective passion, and honestly thought her sons the hand-somest boys she had ever seen anywhere. Murray McCrae, the third child, was a slender dark lad with a closed face and a reserve im-pregnable to all the grown-up world.

"Ralph! Hey there, boys! Here I am, up here."

The children heard the voice and looked around.

"It's Estella, Mama," Ralph said. "There she is, over by the barges."

Sunlight flashed off the water in their eyes. Anna put the tackle box on the fender of the car and, shading her eyes against the glare, pushed her glasses up on her nose and peered toward the terminal.

"Hi, Estella," Steve shouted. He and Ralph put down the poles and cooler and ran down the rough uneven slope of the levee, jump-ing over the huge iron rings that were set in the concrete to hold mooring lines, and over the rusty cables that held the terminal barges against the levee.

"Come on, Murray," Anna said. "Let's go speak to Estella. She's over there fishing off the ramp."

A huge and beautiful Negro woman was sitting on the galvanized iron walkway which ran from the terminal to the levee, her legs dangling over the side of the walkway, ten feet above the oily surface of the water. She held a cane pole in one hand and with the other waved and beckoned toward Anna and the children. Her serene, round face was a creamy golden brown, the skin flawless even in the cruel light of the August sun, her black hair pulled severely back to a knot on her neck, her enormous dark eyes and wide mouth smiling with pleasure at the unexpected meeting. As the children approached, she drew her line out of the water and pulled herself up by the cable that served as a side rail to the walkway. The walk creaked under her shifting weight. She was fully five feet ten inches tall—at least seven inches taller than Anna—and loomed above the heads of the little group on the levee like a goodnatured golden giantess, her feet set wide apart to support the weight that fleshed her big frame. But in spite of her size she did not look fat except around the belly which was still swollen from a recent pregnancy. A gaily flowered house-dress printed with daisies and morning glories in shades of blue, green, and yellow flapped around her legs and stretched tight across her thighs and belly, looking like a robe that some tropical fertility goddess might wear. One would not have been surprised to see a garland of vine leaves in her hair.

Steve ran out on the walkway as if to throw his arms around her, but at the last moment in an access of shyness backed off and said, "Hi, Estella."

"Lord, Estella," Anna said. "Come on down. We haven't seen you in ages. How have you been?"

"You see me," Estella said. "Fat as ever." She wrapped her line around her pole and, shooing Steve ahead of her, came down from her high perch. "Baby or no baby, I got to go fishing after such a fine rain," she said.

"We're going on a picnic," Steve said.

"Well, isn't that fine," Estella said. "Where is Richard?"

"Oh, he thinks he's too old to associate with us any more," Anna said. "He *scorns* us. How is the baby?"

The two women looked at each other with the shy pleasure of old friends long separated who have not yet fallen into the easy ways of their friendship.

"Baby's fine," Estella said. "I left my cousin Bernice nursing him. I said to myself this morning, I haven't been fishing since I got pregnant with Lee Roy. I *got* to go fishing. So look at me. Here I am sitting on this ramp since seven this morning and no luck."

At this point Steve got over his shyness and threw his arms around Estella's legs. "Estella, why don't you come *work* for us again?" he said. "We don't like *anybody* but you."

"I'm coming, honey," she said. "Let me get these kids up a little bit and I'll be back." She turned her attention courteously now to Murray. "How you been, Murray? You still keep up with the Dodgers? I like to took to my bed when I heard they was going to Los Angeles."

Murray bobbed his head, grinned, and said nothing.

"Why don't you go fishing with us today?" Ralph said. "We're going up to the north end of the lake and fish all day."

"Yes, come on," Anna said. "Keep me company. You can't catch any fish around this old barge, and if you do, they taste like fuel oil. I heard the bream are really biting in the upper lake over on the other side, you know, in the willows. Mr. Ferguson told me yesterday he and his wife caught a hundred fish up there in about three hours."

Estella hesitated, looking out over the calm and shining dark water. "I ain't much on boats," she said. "Boats make me nervous."

"Oh, come on, Estella," Anna said. "You know you want to go."

"Well, it's the truth; I'm not catching any fish here. I got two little no 'count bream on my stringer." Estella paused. "*All* y'all going to fish from the boat? I'll crowd you."

"We're going to find a good spot and fish off the bank," Anna said. "We're already too many to fish from the boat."

"Well, it'll be a pleasure," Estella said. "I'll just come along. Let me get my stuff." She crossed the walkway again and gathered up her tackle where it lay—a brown paper sack holding sinkers, floats, hooks and line, her pole, and a coffee can full of dirt and worms.

"I brought my gig," Ralph said, as they trudged across the levee toward the Yacht Club. "I'm going to gig one of those great big buffalo or a gar or something."

"Well, if you do, give it to me, honey," Estella said. "James is really crazy about buffalo the way I cook it." Pulling a coin purse out of her pocket, she turned to Anna. "You reckon you might get us some beer in the Yacht Club? A nice can of beer 'long about eleven o'clock would be good."

"I've got two cans in the cooler," Anna said, "but maybe we'd better get a couple more." She took the money and, while Murray and Ralph brought the skiff around from the far side of the Yacht Club where it was tied up, went into the bar and bought two more cans of beer.

Gaines Williamson, a short, powerfully built Negro man in his forties, followed her out of the bar and helped them stow their gear in the little boat. The children got in first, and then he helped Estella in.

"Lord, Miss Estella," he said, "you too big for this boat, and that's a fact." He stood back and looked down at her doubtfully, sweat shining on his round smooth face and standing in droplets on his shaven scalp.

"I must say, it's none of your business," Estella said.

"We'll be all right, Gaines," Anna said. "The lake's smooth as glass."

The boys held the skiff against the float while Anna got in, and they set out, cruising slowly up the lake until they found a spot that Estella and Anna agreed looked promising. Here, on a long clean sandbar, they beached the boat. The children stripped off their life jackets, pulled off the jeans they wore over their swimming trunks, and began to wade.

"You children wade here in the open water," Estella ordered. "Don't go over yonder on the other side of the bar where the willows are growing. You'll bother the fish."

She and Anna stood looking around. Wilderness was all about them. As far as they could see on either side of the lake not even a road ran down to the water's edge. While they watched, two white herons dragged themselves awkwardly into the air and flapped away, long legs trailing. Green and sand-colored plains, which in the spring had been a part of the bottom of the lake, now swept up and back a quarter of a mile to the rise of the levee. The ground was marked every hundred or so yards with a wavy line like the high-tide line on a beach, which, when one drew closer, turned out to be tangles of driftwood, laid down in undulating bands where the lake had paused in its steady summer drop. Clumps of cottonwood and syca-more trees rose here and there from hummocks of grassy sand which earlier in the summer had been islands in the broad expanse of the lake. Ranks of willows, fringed from top to bottom with delicate, feathery fronds and banded with water marks, thrust their spindly trunks thirty, forty, or fifty feet into the air, taller the farther back they stood from the lake. The southern side of the sandbar had no trees growing on it, but the northern side, which curved in on itself and out again, was covered with willows. Here the land was higher.

Beyond a low hummock crowned with cottonwood trees, Anna and Estella discovered a pool left behind by the last rise. Fringe willows grew all around it, and the fallen trunk of a huge cottonwood lay with its roots exposed on the ground, its whole length stretched out into the still water of the pool.

"Here's the place," Estella said decidedly. "Shade for us and fringe willows for the fish. And looka there." She pointed to the fallen tree. "If there aren't any fish under *there* . . . !" They stood for a few minutes looking at the pool. Then Estella said, "I'll go get our things, Miss Anna. You sit down and rest yourself."

"I'll come help you."

The two women unloaded the boat, and Anna carried the cooler up the low hill and left it in the shade of one of the cottonwood trees. Then they gathered the fishing tackle and took it over to a shady spot by the pool. In a few minutes the children joined them, and Anna passed out poles and bait. The bream were rising to crickets, and she had brought a wire cylinder basket full of them.

"Steve, watch Estella, so you'll know how to do it right," she said. "If you don't get the hook under the hard part of the back, it'll tear out the first time you throw it in the water."

Estella helped Steve bait his hook and then dropped her own into the water as close as she could get it to the trunk of the fallen tree.

"You boys scatter out now," Anna said. "There's plenty of room for everybody, and if you stay too close together you'll hook each other."

Almost as soon as Estella's float struck the water, it began to bob and quiver.

"Here we go," she said in a low voice. "Take it under now. Take it under." She addressed herself to the business of fishing with such delight and concentration that Anna stopped in the middle of rigging a pole to watch her. Even the children, intent on finding places for themselves, turned back to see Estella catch a fish. She stood over the pool like a priestess at her altar, all expectation and willingness, holding the pole lightly, as if her fingers could read the intentions of the fish vibrating through line and pole. Her bare arms were tense and she gazed down into the still water. A puff of wind made the leafy shadows waver and tremble on the pool, and the float rocked deceptively. Estella's arms quivered with a jerk begun and suppressed. Her flowery dress flapped around her legs, and her skin shone with sweat and oil where the sunlight struck through the leaves, across her forehead and down one cheek.

"Not yet," she muttered. "*Take* it." The float bobbed and went under. "Ahh!" She gave her line a quick, short jerk to set the hook, the line tightened, the long pole bent, and she swung a big bream out onto the sand. The fish flopped off the hook and down the slope toward the water; she dropped the pole and dived at it, half falling. Ralph, who had been watching, was ahead of her, shouting with excitement, grabbing the fish before it could flop back into the pool, and putting it into Estella's hands, careful to avoid the sharp dorsal fin.

"Look, boys, look!" she cried happily. "Just look at him." She held out the big bream, as wide and thick as her hand, marked with blue around the gills and orange on its swollen belly. The fish twisted and gasped in her hand while she got the stringer. She slid the metal end of the stringer through the gill and out the mouth, secured it to an exposed root of the fallen tree, and dropped the fish into the water, far enough away so that the bream's thrashing would not disturb their fishing spot.

"Quick now, Miss Anna," she said. "Get your line in there. I bet this pool is full of bream. Come on boys, we're going to catch some fish today."

Anna baited her hook and dropped it in. The children scattered

around the pool to their own places. In an hour the two women had caught a dozen bream and four small catfish, and the boys had caught six or seven more bream. Then for ten minutes no one got a bite, and the boys began to lose interest. A school of minnows flashed into the shallow water at Anna's feet, and she pointed them out to Estella. "Bream are gone," she said. "They've quit feeding, or we wouldn't see any minnows." She laid down her pole and told the children they could swim. "Come on, Estella," she said. "We can sit in the shade and watch them and have a beer, and then in a little while we can move to another spot."

"You aren't going to let them swim in this old lake, are you, Miss Anna?" Estella said.

"Sure. The bottom's nice and sandy here," Anna said. "Murray, your mama said you've got to keep your life preserver on if you swim." She said to Estella in a low voice, "He's not much of a swimmer. He's the only one I would worry about."

The children splashed and tumbled fearlessly in the water, Ralph and Steve popping up and disappearing, sometimes for so long that Anna, in spite of what she had said, would begin to watch anxiously for their blond heads.

"I must say, I don't see how you stand it," Estella said. "That water scares me."

"Nothing to be scared of," Anna said. "They're both good swimmers and so am I. I could swim across the lake and back, I bet you, old as I am." She fished two beers out of the Scotch cooler, opened them, and gave one to Estella. Then she sat down with her back against one of the cottonwood trees, gave Estella a cigarette, took one herself, and leaned back with a sigh. Estella sat down on a fallen log, and the two women smoked and drank their beer in silence for a few minutes. The breeze ran through the cottonwoods, shaking the leaves against each other with a characteristic rainy sound.

"I love the sound of the wind in a cottonwood tree," Anna said. "Especially at night when you wake up and hear it outside your window. I remember there was one outside the window of my room when I was a little girl, so close to the house I could climb out the window and get into it." The breeze freshened and the leaves pattered against each other. "It sounds cool," Anna said, "even in August."

"It's nice," Estella said. "Like a nice, light rain."

"Well, tell me what you've been doing with yourself," Anna said. "When are you going to move into your new house?"

"James wants to keep renting it out another year," Estella said. "He wants us to get ahead a little bit. And you know, Miss Anna, if I can hang on where I am, we'll be in a good shape. We can rent that house until we finish paying for it, and then when we move, we can rent the one we're in, and you know, we own that little one next door, too. With all these children, we got to think of the future. And I must say, with all his old man's ways, James is a good provider. He looks after his own. So I go along with him. But, Lord, I can't stand it much longer. We're falling all over each other in that little tiny place. Kids under my feet all day. No place to keep the baby quiet. And in rainy weather! It's worse than a circus. I've gotten so all I do is yell at the kids. I have done nothing since the baby was born but yell at the kids. It would be a rest to go back to work."

"I wish you *would* come back to work," Anna said.

"No use talking about it," Estella said. "James says I've got to stay home at least until Lee Roy gets up school age. And you can see for yourself, I'd be paying out half what I made to get somebody to keep mine. But I'll tell you, my nerves are tore up."

"It takes a while to get your strength back after a baby," Anna said.

"Oh, I'm strong enough," Estella said. "It's not that."

"Well, Lord knows you've had enough to tear your nerves up," Anna said. "You know you never should have had this last one. Five children are enough for anybody."

"It's the truth," Estella said.

"Of course, it's none of my business, but you ought to go ahead and do what the doctor told you to do before you got pregnant with Lee Roy. Or have you done it already? Got your tubes tied, I mean."

"Miss Anna, I can't come to that," Estella said. "James says it's against nature. And I incline to agree."

"It's against my nature to think about your having any more children," Anna said. "You can't tell me those terrible headaches of yours aren't from the strain of having too many too fast. And you're not young any more. It's just plain too much on you all the time."

"The midwife says Lee Roy is the last," Estella said. "She says she can tell. That I don't need to worry any more."

"Estella!" Anna shook her head impatiently. "Where does the midwife get her information? Does she have a private wire to God?"

"She's had the experience," Estella said stubbornly. "She ought to know."

"Besides, there are other ways," Anna said. "You wouldn't have to get your tubes tied."

"It's all against nature," Estella said. "One way as much as another. And anyhow, you know how a man is. Especially an old man like James. He was late starting his family and it makes him proud for me to bear a child. Every year he wants to get another." She smiled, as if in tolerance of her husband's pride in his virility, and then pulled a stalk of Johnson grass and began to chew it thoughtfully. "I've had something on my mind," she said, "something I've been meaning to tell you ever since the baby came, and I haven't seen you by yourself."

Anna interrupted her. "Look at the fish, Estella," she said. "They're really kicking up a fuss."

There was a wild thrashing commotion in the water by the roots of the cottonwood tree where Estella had tied the stringer.

Estella watched a minute. "Lord, Miss Anna," she said. "Something's after those fish. A turtle or something." She got up and started toward the pool as a long, dark, whiplike shape flung itself out of the water, slapped the surface, and disappeared.

"Hey," Anna said, "it's a snake! A snake!"

Estella looked around for a weapon and hastily picked up a short, heavy stick and a rock from the ground. Moving lightly and easily in spite of her weight, she ran down to the edge of the water, calling over her shoulder, "I'll scare him off. I'll chunk him. Don't you worry." She threw the rock into the churning water, but it had

no effect. "Go, snake. Leave our fish alone." She stood waving her stick threateningly over the water.

Anna came down to the pool now, and they both saw the whip-like form again. Fearlessly Estella whacked at it with her stick.

"Keep back, Estella," Anna said. "He might bite you. Wait a minute and I'll get a longer stick."

"Go, snake," Estella shouted furiously, confidently, as if she could command the snake to vanish. "What's the matter with him? He won't go off. Go, you crazy snake!"

Now the children heard the excitement and came running across the beach and over the low hill where Estella and Anna had been sitting.

"A snake, a snake," Steve screamed. "He's after the fish. Come on y'all."

The two older boys ran up. "Get 'em out of the water, Mama," Ralph said. "He's going to eat 'em."

"I'm scared he might bite me," Anna said. "Keep back. He'll go away in a minute." She struck at the water with the stick she had picked up.

Murray looked the situation over calmly. "Why don't we gig him?" he said to Ralph.

Ralph ran down to the boat and brought back the long, barb-pointed gig. "Move, Estella," he said. "I'm gonna gig him." He struck twice at the snake and missed.

"Estella," Anna said, "I saw his head. He can't go away. He's swallowed one of the fish. He's caught on the stringer." She shuddered with disgust. "What are we going to do?" she said. "Let's throw away the stringer. We'll never get him off."

"All them beautiful fish! No *ma'am,*" Estella said. "Here, Ralph, he can't bite us if he's swallowed a fish. I'll untie the stringer and get him up on land, and then you gig him."

"I'm going away," Steve said. "I don't want to watch." He crossed the hill and went back to the beach, where he sat down alone and began to dig a hole in the sand.

Ralph was wild with excitement and danced impatiently around Estella while she untied the stringer.

"Be calm, child," she said. She pulled the stringer out of the water and dropped it on the ground. "Now!"

The snake had indeed tried to swallow one of the bream on the stringer; its jaws were stretched so wide as to look dislocated; its body was distended behind the head with the half-swallowed meal, and the fish's head could still be seen protruding from its mouth. The snake, faintly banded with slaty black on a brown background, was a water moccasin.

"Lord, it's a cottonmouth!" Estella cried as soon as she had the stringer out on land where she could see it.

A thrill of horror and disgust raised the hair on Anna's arms. The thought of the helpless fish on the stringer sensing the approach of its enemy, and now, of the snake equally and even more grotesquely helpless, filled her with revulsion. "Throw it away," she commanded. And then the thought of the stringer with its living burden of fish and snake struggling and swimming away into the lake struck her as even worse. "No!" she said. "Go on. Kill the snake, Ralph."

Ralph paid no attention to his mother, but stood with the long gig poised, looking up at Estella for instructions.

"Kill him," Estella said. "Now."

He drove the gig into the snake's body behind the head and pinned it to the ground where it coiled convulsively, wrapping and unwrapping its tail around the gig, and lashing the sand.

Anna mastered herself as well as she could. "Now what?" she said calmly.

Estella got a knife from the tackle box, held down the dead but still writhing snake, with one foot behind the gig on its body and the other on its tail, squatted, and deftly cut off the fish's head where it protruded from the gaping, fanged mouth. Then she worked the barbed point of the gig out of the body, picked the snake up on the point, and stood holding it away from her. Ralph whirled around with excitement, and circled Estella twice. "We've killed a snake," he chanted. "We've killed a snake. We've killed a snake."

"Look at it wiggle," Murray said. "It keeps on wiggling even after it's dead."

"Yeah, a snake'll wiggle like that for an hour sometimes, even with its head cut off," Estella said. "Look out, Ralph." She swept the gig forward and threw the snake out into the pool, where it continued its mindless writhing on the surface of the water. She handed Ralph the gig and stood watching the snake for a few minutes, holding her hands away from her sides to keep the blood off her clothes. Then she bent down by the water's edge and washed the blood from her hands. "There!" she said. "I didn't have no idea of th'owing away all them, *those* beautiful fish. James would've skinned me, if he ever heard about it."

Steve got up from the sand now and came over to his mother. He looked at the writhing snake and then he leaned against his mother without saying anything, put his arms around her, and laid his head against her side.

Anna stroked his hair with one hand and held him close to her with the other. "It was a moccasin, honey," she said. "They're poison, you know. You have to kill them."

"I'm hungry," Ralph said. "Is it time to eat?"

Anna shook her head, gave Steve a pat, and released him. "Let me smoke a cigarette first and forget about that old snake. Then we'll eat."

She and Estella went back to the shade on the hill and settled themselves once more, each with a fresh can of beer and a cigarette. The children returned to the beach.

"I can do without snakes," Anna said. "Indefinitely."

Estella was still breathing hard. "I don't mind killing no snake," she said happily.

"I never saw anything like that before," Anna said. "A snake getting caught on a stringer, I mean. Did you?"

"Once or twice," Estella said. "And I've had 'em get after my stringer plenty of times."

"I don't see how you could stand to cut the fish's head off." Anna shivered.

"Well, somebody had to."

"Yes, I suppose I would have done it, if you hadn't been here." She laughed. "*Maybe*. I was mighty tempted to throw the whole thing away."

"I'm just as glad I wasn't pregnant," Estella said. "I'm glad it didn't happen while I was carrying Lee Roy. I would have been *helpless*."

"You might have had a miscarriage," Anna said. She laughed again, still nervous, wanting to stop talking about the snake, but feeling somehow that there was more to be said, something that would banish her sense of the ritual unreality of the scene. "Please don't have any miscarriages on fishing trips with me," she said. "I can do without that, too."

"Miscarriage!" Estella said. "That's not what I'm talking about. And that reminds me, what I was getting ready to tell you when we saw the snake. You know, I said I had something on my mind?"

"Uh-huh."

"You remember last summer when you weren't home that day, and that kid fell out of the tree in the yard, and all?"

"How could I forget it?"

"You remember you spoke to me so heavy about it? Why didn't I stay out in the yard with him until his mama got there instead of leaving him laying on the ground like that, nobody with him but the boys, and I told you I couldn't go out there to him, couldn't look at that kid with his leg broke and all, and you didn't understand why?"

"Yes, I remember," Anna said.

"Well, I wanted to tell you I was *blameless,*" Estella said. "I didn't want you to know it at the time, but I was pregnant. I *couldn't* go out there."

"I reckon you were," Anna said. "I hadn't realized it. But what does that have to do with it?"

Estella looked at her impatiently. "I was pregnant," she repeated.

"Were you sick or something?"

"It might have *marked* my child, don't you see? I might have bore a cripple."

"Oh, Estella! You don't believe that kind of foolishness, do you?" Anna said.

"Believe it! I've seen it happen," Estella said. "I know it's true." She was sitting on the fallen log so that she towered above Anna, who had gone back to her place on the ground, leaning against a tree. Now she leaned forward with an expression of intense seriousness on her face. "My aunt looked on a two-headed calf when she was carrying a child," she said, "and her child had six fingers on one hand and seven on the other."

Anna hitched herself up higher, then got up and sat down on the log beside Estella. "But that was an accident," she said, "a coincidence. Looking at the calf didn't have anything to do with it."

Estella shook her head stubbornly. "This world is a mysterious place," she said. "Do you think you can understand everything in it?"

"No," Anna said. "Not everything. But I don't believe in magic."

"All this world is full of mystery," Estella repeated. "You got to have respect for what you don't understand. There are times to be brave and times when you go down helpless in spite of all. Like that snake. You were afraid of that snake."

"I thought he might bite me," Anna said. "And besides, it was so horrible the way he was caught."

But Estella went on as if she had not heard. "You see," she said, "there are things you overlook. Things like I was telling you about my aunt that are *true*. My mother in her day saw more wonders than that. She knew more than one that sickened and died of a spell. And this child with the fingers, I know about him for a fact. I lived with them when I was teaching school. I lived in the house with that kid. So I'm not taking any chances."

"But I thought you had lost your head and gotten scared because he was hurt," Anna said. "When the little boy broke his leg, I mean. I kept thinking it wasn't like you. That's what really happened, isn't it?"

"No," Estella said. "It was like I told you."

Anna said no more, but sat quiet a long time, lighting another cigarette and smoking calmly, her face expressionless. But her thoughts were in a tumult of exasperation, bafflement, and outrage. She tried unsuccessfully to deny, to block out the overriding sense of the difference between herself and Estella, borne in on her by this conversation, so foreign to their quiet, sensible friendship. She had often thought, with pride both in herself and in Estella, what an accomplishment their friendship was, knowing how much delicacy of feeling, how much consideration and understanding they had both brought to it. "Maybe," Anna had told herself many times, "it's because she's so *big*. Anybody that big, black or white, would have to be magnanimous. Why, she could break me in half if she liked.

And James, too, for that matter." And she had laughed at the thought of Estella turning on the slender, graying husband who ruled his house like an old-fashioned patriarch, and holding him helpless in the circle of her huge, golden arms.

But Anna did not give all the credit for the friendship to Estella. She had resolved from the beginning to wipe out, at least in this one small area of her own personal life, the universal guilt, the heritage that builds itself every day into a more complex and hate-filled present. With innocent virtue she had determined to be born again and baptized with the purity of her own motives. And now it seemed to her that it was this very resolve that Estella, from within the magic circle she had drawn about herself, attacked. With a few words she had put between them all that separated them, all the dark and terrible past. Anna was filled with a horror and confusion incommensurate with the commonplace superstitions that Estella had stated in confident expectation of understanding and acceptance. It was as if a chasm had opened between them from which there rose, like fog off the nightmare waters of a dream, the wisps and trails of misted feelings: hates she had thought exorcised, contempt she had believed rendered contemptible, the power that corrupts and the submission that envenoms.

In the tumult of her feelings there rose a queer, long-forgotten memory of a nurse she had once had as a child—the memory of a brown hand thrust out at her holding a greasy ball of hair combings: "You see, child, I saves my hair. I ain't never th'owed away a hair of my head."

"Why?" she had asked.

"Bad luck to th'ow away combings. Bad luck to lose any part of yourself in this old world. Fingernail parings, too. I gathers them up, and carries them home and burns them. And I sits by the fire and watches until every last little bitty hair is turned plumb to smoke."

"But why?" she had asked again.

"Let your enemy possess one hair of your head and you will be in his power," the nurse had said. She had thrust the hair ball into her apron pocket, and now, in the memory, she seemed to be brushing Anna's hair, and Anna remembered standing restive under her hand, hating as always, to have her hair brushed.

"Hurry up," she had said. "I got to go."

"All right, honey. I'm th'ough." The nurse had given her head one last lick, and then, bending toward her, still holding her arm while she struggled to be off and outdoors again, had thrust a dark, brooding face close to hers, had looked at her for a long, scary moment, and then had laughed. "I saves your combings, too, honey. You in my power."

And there were tribes—where had she read of them?—whose members all their lives kept their own dried and shriveled afterbirths in pouches tied about their necks. With an effort she drew herself up short. What did all this have to do with her, or with Estella, the lovely, tranquil Estella with her calm efficiency, her clear, Palmer-method handwriting, her forceful, schoolteacherish ways. "But that's part of the difference," she thought, remembering when and where Estella had taught. The two women were within a year of the same age, and when she, Anna, had been in the ninth grade, a child with no more responsibilites laid on her than a grasshopper, Estella had been teaching the first grade in a little country school outside of Vicksburg. By the time Anna had received her first dry, timid kiss from a downy-cheeked boy-child, Estella had a lover. Already carrying his child, she had been married at fifteen, and had, besides the four young children who were James's, a grown son and daughter by this early marriage.

But there was nothing to be said about any of this—either Estella's life or her own—no way to bring about the fusion of background and feeling that occasionally happens between two people, so that it seems for a little space of time that each has available all the experience and understanding of the other, and senses in himself the sources of all the other's fears and failures.

She put out her cigarette, threw her beer can into the lake, and stood up. "I reckon we'd better fix lunch," she said. "The children are starving. We can try another fishing spot after we eat."

III

BY THE TIME they had finished lunch, burned the discarded papers, thrown the bread crusts and crumbs of potato chips to the birds, and put the empty soft-drink bottles back into the cooler, it had begun to look like rain. Anna stood gazing thoughtfully into the sky. Here on the sandbar it was still sunny; but the breeze had freshened and the surface of the lake was choppy. Far away in the south, dark rain clouds were blowing along the horizon, driving before them the gray veil of a rain squall.

"Maybe we ought to start back," Anna said. "We don't want to get caught in the rain up here."

"We're not going to catch any more fish as long as the wind is blowing," Estella said.

"We want to swim some more," Ralph said.

"You can't go swimming right after lunch," Anna said. "You might get a cramp. And it won't be any fun to get caught in the rain. We'd better call it a day." She picked up one of the poles and began to wind the line around it. "Come on, let's load up. Fix the poles right, now. Wrap the lines tight and stick the hooks in the corks, and don't anybody leave his bait on his hook."

They loaded their gear into the skiff. Anna directed Murray and Steve to sit in the bow, Estella got cautiously in and took the middle seat, Anna and Ralph waded in together, pushed the skiff off the sandbar, turned it around, and got into the stern.

"Have you all got your life jackets on?" Anna glanced at the boys. "That's right, Murray, pull the bottom strap tight, and buckle it."

Ralph pulled on the recoil starter rope until he had got the little motor started, and they headed down the lake. The heavily loaded skiff showed no more than eight inches of freeboard, and as they cut through the choppy water, waves sprayed over the bow and sprinkled Murray and Steve. Steve began to drag his hand in the water so its wake would splash Estella.

"Stop that, Steve. Don't let's get any wetter than we have to," Anna said. She moved the tiller and headed the skiff in closer to the shore. "We'll stay close in going down," she said. "The water's not so rough. And we can cut across the lake right opposite the Yacht Club."

Anna's heart beat heavily with the excitement and brilliance of the day. No place in the world, she thought, are clouds so beautiful as here. Maybe because everything else is so level and green, you can concentrate on the sky. Thunderheads, tumbled by the wind into breathtaking white mountains against the blue heavens, were shot through with motey sunbeams, their flat bases shadowed on the undersides with layers of pale and darkly bluish gray, mauve, violet, and even, where the light struck through behind them, a kind of pale, vanishing rose. Sheets of rapidly shifting light and shadow from the rushing sky raced across the water, changing it from spark-shot green to steel green to steel gray to black.

"I don't like this old lake when it's windy," Estella said. "I don't like no windy water." She sat rigid in the middle of the skiff, her back to Anna, a hand on each gunwale, as they moved down the lake, bouncing and rocking with the waves.

When they reached a point opposite the Yacht Club, Anna headed the skiff into the open water. Here the lake was a little more than a mile wide. All the way down, they had been traveling from west to east, as the northern arm of the horseshoe-shaped lake lay oriented almost directly east and west. They had now reached the bend of the horseshoe, with the Philippi lakefront, terminal, and Yacht Club on its eastern shore. South of Philippi the southern arm of the horseshoe, the channel opening into the river, lay southwest to northeast, so that the wind, instead of being cut off by the protection of the levee, as it had been in the upper lake, blew with all its un-broken force straight up the open channel. The wind, however, was still no more than a stiff breeze, and the skiff was a quarter of the way across the lake before Anna began to be worried. Spray from the choppy waves was coming in more and more often over the bow, Murray and Steve were drenched, and an inch of water sloshed in the bottom of the skiff. Estella had not spoken since she had said, "I don't like no windy water." She sat perfectly still, gripping the gun-wales with both hands, her paper sack of tackle in her lap, her worm can on the seat beside her. Suddenly a gust of wind picked up the paper sack and blew it out of the boat. It struck the water and floated back to Anna, who reached out, picked it up, and dropped it by her own feet. Estella did not move, although the sack had brushed against her face as it blew out. She made no move to catch it.

She's scared, Anna thought, She's so scared she didn't even see it blow away; and Anna was frightened herself. She leaned forward, picked up the worm can from the seat beside Estella, dumped out the worms and dirt, and tapped Estella on the shoulder. "Here," she said. "Bail some of the water out of the bottom of the boat, so your feet won't get wet."

Estella did not look around, but reached over her shoulder, took the can, and began to bail, still holding the gunwale tightly with her left hand.

The wind blew, the waves began to show white at their tips, the clouds in the south raced across the sky, darker and darker. But still, although they could see sheets of rain far away to the south, the sun shone on them brightly. They were now almost halfway across the lake. Anna looked over her shoulder toward the quieter water they had left behind. Along the shore of the lake the willow trees tossed in the wind, like a forest of green plumes.

It's just as far one way as the other, she thought, and anyhow there's nothing to be afraid of. But while she looked back, the boat slipped off course, no longer quartering the waves, and immediately they took a big one over their bow.

"Bail, Estella," Anna said quietly, putting the boat back on course. "Get that water out of the boat." Her mind was filled with one paralyzing thought: She can't swim. My God, Estella can't swim.

Far off down the channel she saw the *Gay Rosey Jane* moving steadily toward the terminal, pushing a string of barges. She looked at Murray and Steve in the bow of the boat, drenched, hair plastered to their heads.

"Just sit still, boys," she said. "There's nothing to worry about. We're almost there."

The wind was a gale now and the black southern sky rushed toward them as if to engulf them. The boat took another wave over the bow and then another. Estella bailed mechanically with the coffee can. They were still almost half a mile out from the Yacht Club.

The boat's overloaded and we're going to sink, Anna thought. My God, we're going to sink, and Estella can't swim.

"Estella," she said, "the boat will not sink. It may fill up with water, but it won't sink. Do you understand? It is all filled with cork like a life preserver. It *won't sink,* do you hear me?" She repeated herself louder and louder above the wind. Estella sat with her back turned and bailed. She did not move or answer or even nod her head. She went on bailing frantically, mechanically, dumping pint after pint of water over the side, while they continued to ship waves over the bow.

Murray and Steve sat in their places and stared at Anna. Ralph sat motionless by her side. No one said a word.

I've got to take care of them all, Anna thought. "Estella," she said, "don't panic. Keep perfectly still and you'll be all right. The boat won't sink. You can stay in it, even if it is full of water, and it will hold you up. Do you hear me? Keep still and don't panic."

The boat settled in the water and shipped another wave, wallowing now, hardly moving before the labored push of the motor. Estella gave a yell and started to rise, holding to the gunwales with both hands.

"Sit down, you fool!" Anna shouted. "*Sit down!*"

"We're gonna sink!" Estella yelled. "And I can't swim, Miss Anna! I can't swim!" For the first time she turned and stared at Anna with wild, blind eyes. She stood all the way up and clutched the air. "I'm gonna drown!" she yelled.

The boat rocked and settled, the motor drowned out, another wave washed in over the bow, and the boat tipped slowly up on its side. An instant later they were all in the water and the boat was floating upside down beside them.

The children bobbed up immediately, buoyant in their life jackets. Anna glanced around once to see if they were all there.

"Stay close to the boat, boys," she said.

And then Estella heaved out of the water, fighting frantically, eyes vacant, mouth open, the broad expanse of her golden face set in mindless desperation. Anna got hold of one of the hand grips at the stern of the boat and with her free hand grabbed Estella's arm.

"You're all right," she said. "Come on, I've got hold of the boat."

She tried to pull the huge bulk of the Negro woman toward her and guide her hand to the grip. Estella did not speak, but lunged forward in the water with a strangled yell and threw herself on Anna, flinging her arms across her shoulders. Anna felt herself sinking and scissors-kicked strongly to keep herself up, but she went down. Chin-deep in the water, she threw back her head and took a breath before Estella pushed her under. She hung on to the grip with all her strength, feeling herself battered against the boat and jerked away from it by Estella's struggle.

This can't be happening, she thought. We can't be out here drowning. She felt a frantic hand brush across her face and snatch at her nose and hair. My glasses, she thought as she felt them torn away. I've lost my glasses.

Estella's weight slid away and she, too, went under. Then both women came up and Anna got hold of Estella's arm again.

"Come *on*," she gasped. "The *boat*."

Again Estella threw herself forward, the water streaming from her head and shoulders. This time Anna pulled her close enough to get hold of the grip, but Estella did not try to grasp it. Her hand slid clawing along Anna's wrist and arm; again she somehow rose up in the water and came down on Anna, and again the two women went under. This time Estella's whole thrashing bulk was above Anna; she held with all her strength to the hand grip, but felt herself torn away from it. She came up behind Estella, who was now clawing frantically at the side of the skiff, which sank down on their side and tipped gently toward them as she pulled at it.

She won't do *anything,* Anna thought. I can't make her help herself. And then: Maybe I can get her up on it.

She ducked down and somehow got her shoulder against Estella's rump. Kicking and heaving with a strength she did not possess, she boosted Estella up and forward so that she fell sprawling across the boat. "*There!*" She came up as the rocking skiff began to submerge under Estella's weight. "Stay there!" she gasped. "*Stay* on it! For God's . . ."

But the boat was under a foot of water now, rocking and slipping away under Estella's shifting weight. Clutching and kicking crazily, mouth open in a soundless, prolonged scream, eyes staring, she slipped off the other side, turned her face toward Anna, gave a strange, strangled grunt, and sank again. The water churned and foamed where she had been.

Anna swam around the boat toward her. As she swam, she realized that Ralph and Steve were screaming for help. Murray floated in the water with a queer, embarrassed smile on his face, as if he had been caught at something shameful. I'm not here, he seemed to be saying. This is all just an embarrassing mistake.

By the time Anna got to Estella, the boat was a couple of yards away, too far, she knew, for her to try to get Estella back to it. Estella broke the surface of the water directly in front of her, and immediately flung both arms around her neck. Nothing she had ever learned in a lifesaving class seemed to have any bearing on this reasonless two hundred pounds of flesh with which she had to deal. They went down. This time they stayed under so long, deep in the softly yielding black water, that Anna thought she would not make it up. Her very brain seemed ready to burst out of her ears and nostrils. She scissors-kicked again and again with all her strength, not trying to pull loose from Estella's clinging, but now more passive weight, and they came up. Anna's head was thrust up and back, ready for a breath, and the instant she felt the air on her face, she took it, deep and gulping, swallowing some water at the same time, and they went down again. Estella's arms rested heavily, trustingly, it seemed, on her shoulders. She did not try to hug Anna or strangle her, but simply kept holding on and pushing her down. This time, again deep in the dark water, when Anna raised her arms for a strong downstroke to send them up, she touched a foot. One of the boys was floating above their heads. She grabbed the foot without a thought, and pulled with all her strength, scissors-kicking at the same time. They popped out of the water. Gasping in the life-giving air, Anna found herself staring into Steve's face as he floated beside her, weeping.

My God, I'll drown him if he doesn't get out of the way, she thought. I'll drown my own child. But she had no time to say even a word to warn him off before they went down again.

The next time up she heard Ralph's voice, high and shrill and almost in her ear, and realized that he, too, was swimming close by, and was pounding on Estella's shoulder. "Estella, let go, let go!" he was crying. "Estella, you're drowning Mama!" Estella did not hear. She seemed not even to try to raise her head or breathe when their heads broke out of the water. Her mouth stayed open and the water sloshed into it and rattled in her throat. Her feet kicked aimlessly and still she kept her arms gently, trustingly around Anna's neck, and pulled her down.

Once more they went under and came up before Anna thought,

I've given out. There's no way to keep her up, and nobody is coming. And then, deep in the lake, the brassy taste of fear on her tongue, the yielding water pounding in her ears, *She's going to drown me. I've got to let her drown, or she will drown me.* She drew her knee up under her chin, planted her foot in the soft belly, still swollen from pregnancy, and shoved as hard as she could, pushing herself up and back, and Estella down and away. It was easy to push her away. The big arms slid off Anna's shoulders, the limp hands making no attempt to clutch or hold. They had been together, close as lovers in the darkness or as twins in the womb of the lake, and now they were apart. Anna shot up into the air with the force of her shove and took a deep, gasping breath. Treading water, she waited for Estella to come up beside her, but nothing happened. The three children floated in a circle and looked at her. A vision passed through her mind of Estella's body drifting downward through layers of increasing darkness, all her golden strength and flowery beauty mud- and water-dimmed, still, aimless as a drifting log. She reached down and felt all around her with hands and feet. I ought to surface-dive and look for her, she thought, and the thought of going down again turned her bowels to water.

Before she had to decide to dive, something nudged lightly against her hand, like an inquiring, curious fish. She grabbed at it and felt the inert mass of Estella's body, drained of struggle, floating below the surface of the water. She got hold of the cloth of her dress and pulled. Estella's back broke the surface of the water, mounded and rocking in the dead man's float, and then sank gently down again. Anna took hold of her belt and moved her feet tiredly to keep herself afloat. I can't even get her face out of the water, she thought. I haven't the strength to lift her head.

The boat was floating ten yards away. The Scotch cooler, bright red-and-black plaid, bobbed gaily in the water nearby. Far, far off she could see the levee. In the boat, it had looked so near, and the distance across the lake so little that she had said she could easily swim it, but now everything in the world except the boat, the children, and this lifeless body was unthinkably far away. Tiny black figures moved back and forth along the levee, people going about their business without a thought of tragedy. The whole sweep of the lake was empty, not another boat in sight except the *Gay Rosey Jane*, still moving up the channel. All that had happened had happened so quickly that the towboat seemed no nearer than it had before the skiff overturned. Murray floated in the water a few yards off, still smiling his embarrassed smile. Steve and Ralph stared at their mother with stricken faces. The sun broke through the shifting blackness of the sky, and at the same time a light rain began to fall, pattering on the choppy surface of the lake and splashing into their faces. Still the wind blew and cloud shadows raced across the glittering water.

All her senses dulled and muffled by shock and exhaustion, Anna moved her feet and worked her way toward the boat, dragging her burden.

"She's gone," Steve said. "Estella's drowned." Tears and rain streamed down his face.

"What shall we do, Mama?" Ralph said.

Dimly Anna realized that he had sensed her exhaustion and was trying to rouse her. "Yell," she said. "All three of you. Maybe somebody . . ."

The children screamed for help again and again, their thin, piping voices floating away in the wind. With her last strength, Anna continued to work her way toward the boat pulling Estella after her. She swam on her back, frog-kicking, and feeling the inert bulk bump against her legs with every stroke. When she reached the boat, she took hold of the handgrip and concentrated on holding on to it.

"What shall we do?" Ralph said again. "They can't hear us."

Overcome with despair, Anna let her head droop toward the water. "No one is coming," she said. "It's too far. They can't hear you." And then, from somewhere, dim thoughts of artificial respiration, of snatching back the dead came into her mind and she raised her head. Still time; I've got to get her out *now*, she thought. "Yell again," she said.

"I'm going to swim to shore and get help," Ralph said. He looked toward his mother for a decision, but his face showed clearly that he knew he could not expect one. He started swimming away, his blond head bobbing in the rough water. He did not falter or look back.

"I don't know," Anna said. Then she remembered vaguely that in an accident you were supposed to stay with the boat. She's dead, she said to herself. My God, she's dead. My fault.

Ralph swam on, the beloved head smaller and smaller on the vast expanse of the lake. The *Gay Rosey Jane* moved steadily up the channel.

They might run him down, Anna thought. They'd never see him. She opened her mouth to call him back.

"Somebody's coming!" Murray shouted. "They see us. Somebody's coming. Ralph!"

Ralph heard him and turned back, and now they saw two boats racing toward them, one from the Yacht Club and one from the far side of the lake below and across from the terminal. In the nearer one they saw Gaines Williamson.

Fifty yards away something happened to his engine—it raced, ground, and died. Standing in the stern of the rocking boat, he worked over it frantically while they floated and watched. It could not have been more than a minute or two before the other boat pulled up beside them, but every moment that passed, Anna knew, might be the moment of Estella's death. Now, in the stern of the second boat, they saw a slight, wiry white man wearing a tee shirt and jeans. He cut his engine when he was beside them, and, moving quickly to the side of the boat nearest Anna, bent over her. His voice, when he spoke, was deep and hesitant and he spoke carefully, like one who has with difficulty overcome a stammer.

"Are you all right?" he asked. He grabbed her arm with a hard, calloused hand and shook her, as if he had seen that she was about to pass out. "Are you all right?" he asked again, his face close to hers.

Anna stared at him, scarcely understanding what the question meant. The children swam over to the boat and he helped them in and then turned back to Anna.

"Come on," he said and took hold of her arm again. "You've got to help yourself. Can you make it?"

"Get this one first," she said.

"What?" He stared at her with a queer concentrated gaze, and she realized that he had not even seen Estella. She hauled on the belt and Estella's back broke the surface of the water, rolling, rocking, and bumping against the side of the boat.

"I've got somebody else here," she said.

He grunted as if someone had hit him in the stomach. Reaching down, he grabbed the back of Estella's dress, pulled the body toward him, got one hand into her hair, raised her face out of the water, and, bracing himself against the gunwale, held her there. Estella's peaceful, sleeping face turned slowly toward him. Her mouth and eyes were closed, her expression one of deep repose. The man stared at her and then at Anna. "My God," he said.

"We've got to get her into the boat," Anna said. "If we can get her where we can give her artificial respiration . . ."

"It's Estella," Steve said. "Mama had her all the time."

The three children shifted all at once to the side of the boat where the man was still holding Estella, and the boat tipped crazily.

"Get back," he said gently, still staring at Estella. When they did not obey, he turned on them sternly. "Sit *down*. And sit still."

The children scuttled back to their places, and Steve began to cry again. "Let go of her hair," he said. "You're hurting her."

"It's all right, son," the man said. "She can't feel a thing." To Anna, in a lower voice, he said, "She's dead."

"I'll push and you pull," Anna said. "Maybe we can get her into the boat."

He shifted his position, bracing himself as well as he could in the rocking boat, rested Estella's head on his own shoulder, and put both arms around her. They heaved and pushed at the limp body, weightless as a feather so long as it had been floating underwater, but utterly unmanageable in the air. They could not get her into the boat. The man let her down into the water again, this time holding her under the arms. Her head flopped forward into the water, and he took hold of her hair and raised it up. A hundred yards away Gaines still struggled with his engine.

"Hurry up!" the white man shouted. "Get on over here. We can't lift this woman by ourselves."

"Fishing lines tangled in the screw," Gaines shouted back. His engine caught and died.

"We're going to have to tow her in," the man said. "That fellow can't start his boat." It did not occur to either of them that they could start up the boat and maneuver it near enough to Gaines's boat so that he could help them.

"Hurry," Anna said. "Please hurry." It seemed to her that hours had passed since the white man's boat had pulled up beside them.

"We'd better put this on her first," he said, reaching behind him for a life jacket. They worked her arms into the jacket and fastened the straps. "I've got a rope here somewhere," he said. "Hold her a minute." He laid the sleeping head back against the collar of the jacket and turned away to get his rope. Just then Gaines got his engine started, raced across the water and drew up beside them.

The two boats rocked in the rough water with Anna and Estella between them. Anna, with a hand on the gunwale of each, held them apart while the white man and the powerful Negro, grunting and straining, hauled Estella's body up out of the water and over the gunwale of Gaines's boat. She flopped face down across the seat and lay with one arm hanging over the side, the hand trailing in the water. Anna lifted the arm and put it in the boat. Then the white man pulled Anna into his boat. As he helped her over the side, she heard a smacking blow, and looking back, saw that Gaines had raised and turned Estella's body and was pounding her in the belly. Water poured out of her mouth, and in reflex air rushed in. He flopped her over again, on her stomach, started the engine, and kept it going with one hand (for something still seemed to be wrong with it) while with the other, leaning forward, he pushed on Estella's back in a makeshift effort at artificial respiration. Anna dropped down in the bottom of the boat and lay still.

The boats roared off across the lake toward the Yacht Club. The white man's was much the faster of the two, and he quickly pulled away. As soon as they were within calling distance, he stood up in the boat and began to yell at the little group gathered on the Yacht Club mooring float.

"Drowned! She's drowned! Call an ambulance. Get a resuscitator down here. Hurry!"

They drew up to the float; he threw a rope to one of the Negroes standing there, and jumped out. Anna dragged herself to a sitting position and stared stupidly at the crowd of Negroes. Gaines Williamson pulled up behind them in the other boat.

"Give us a hand," the white man said. "Let's get her out of here. My God, she's huge. Somebody lend a hand."

To Anna it seemed that all the rest of the scene on the float took place above and far away from her. She saw legs moving back and forth, heard voices, snatches of conversation, felt herself moved from one place to another, but nothing that happened interrupted her absorption in grief and guilt. For the time nothing existed except the knowledge that Estella was dead.

Someone took her arm and helped her onto the float while the children climbed up by themselves. She sat down on the splintery boards, surrounded by legs, and no one paid any attention to her.

"I saw 'em." The voice of a Negro woman in the crowd. "I was setting on the levee and I saw 'em. You heard me. 'My Lord save us, some folks out there drowning,' I said. I was up on the levee and I ran down to the Yacht Club . . ."

"Did somebody call an ambulance?" the white man asked.

"I run down here to the Yacht Club, like to killed myself running, and . . ."

"How . . ?"

"*Gay Rosey Jane* swamped them. Never even seen them. Them towboats don't stop for nobody. See, there she goes. Never seen them at all."

"Still got a stitch in my side. My Lord, I like to killed myself running."

"Anybody around here know how to give artificial respiration?"

"I was sitting right yonder on the terminal fishing with her this morning. Would you believe that?"

"God have mercy on us."

"Oh, Lord. Oh, Lord God. Lord God."

"Have mercy on us."

A young Negro man walked over to where the white man and Gaines Williamson were trying to get Estella out of the bulky life jacket. "We'll cut it off," he said calmly. He pulled a straight-edged razor from his pocket, slit one shoulder and the side of the life jacket, pushed it out of the way, and straddled Estella's body. "I know how," he said. "I learned in the Army." He arranged her body in the correct position, lying flat on her stomach, face turned to the side and arms above her head, and set to work, raising her arms and then her body rhythmically. When he lifted her body in the middle, her face dragged on the splintery planks of the float.

Anna crawled through the crowd to where Estella lay. Squatting down without a word, she put her hands under Estella's face to protect it from the splinters. It passed through her mind that she should do something about the children. Looking around, she saw them standing in a row against the Yacht Club wall, staring down at her and Estella, no longer crying, just standing and staring. Somebody ought to get them away from here, she thought vaguely, but the thought left her mind and she forgot them. She swayed, rocked back on her heels, sat down suddenly, and then lay on her stomach, her head against Estella's head, her hands cradling the sleeping face.

Who's going to tell James? she thought. Who's going to tell him she's dead? And then, I have to tell him. She began to talk to Estella. "Please, darling," she said, "please, Estella, breathe." Tears of weakness rolled down her face, and she looked up above the forest of legs at the black faces in a circle around them. "She's got four babies," she said. "*Babies.* Who's going to tell her husband she's dead? Who's going to tell him?" And then, again, "Please, Estella, breathe. Please breathe."

No one answered. The young Negro soldier continued to raise the limp arms and body alternately, his motions deliberate and rhythmical, the sweat pouring off his face and dripping down on his sweat-soaked shirt. His thin face was intent and stern. The storm was over, the clouds had blown away to the west, and the sun had come out and beat down bright and hot, raising steamy air from the rain-soaked float.

The crowd watched, murmuring.

"Lord help us."

"Sweet Lord Jesus have mercy on us."

Ralph squirmed through the crowd and tapped his mother on the shoulder. "Mama, hadn't I better call Daddy?" he said.

"No," she said. "Don't call him. What's the use in calling him?" He would not have to know, she thought, hazily. Above all, James would not have to know. If Richard found out, then surely James would find out, too, and so, if they did not call Richard, James would not know. "Where's the ambulance?" she said. "Why don't they get here with the resuscitator?"

A long time passed. The soldier looked around at the crowd. "Anybody here can spell me?" he asked. "I'm about to give out." He did not pause or break the rhythm of his motions.

A man stepped out of the crowd. "I know how to do it," he said.

"Come on, then, get down here by me and do it with me three times, and then when I stop you take over. Don't break it."

"*Please*, Estella," Anna said.

"One, two . . ."

She felt someone pulling at her arm and looked up. A policeman was standing over her. "Here, lady," he said, "get up off that dock. You ain't doing no good."

"But the splinters will get in her face," Anna said. "I'm holding her face off the boards."

"It ain't going to matter if her face is tore up, if she's dead," the policeman said. "Get up."

By this time the crowd on the float was larger. Fifteen or twenty Negroes were staring at Estella's body, two policemen had come down, and several white men had joined the crowd. Anna looked around at them all, and everyone, it seemed to her, avoided her eyes in embarrassment. But someone handed her a towel and she folded it and put it under Estella's face. The policeman dragged her to her feet and took her over to a chair and sat her down in it. He squatted beside her. "Now, who was in the boat?" he said. "I got to make a report."

Anna made a vague gesture. "*We* were," she said.

"Who is 'we,' lady?"

"Estella and I and the children."

"Lady, give me the names, please," the policeman said.

"Estella Moseby, the Negro woman. She used to work for me, and we *asked* her, we invited her . . ." She broke off.

"Come on, who else?"

Anna stared at him, a short, bald man with shining pink scalp, and drum belly buttoned tightly into his uniform. A wave of nausea overcame her and she saw his head surrounded by the shimmering black spokes of a rimless wheel, a black halo. "I'm going to be sick," she said, and, collapsing out of the chair onto the dock, leaned her head over the edge and vomited into the lake.

He waited until she was through and then helped her back into her chair. "Who else was with you?" he said.

"My two children, Ralph and Steve," she said. "Murray McCrae. I am Mrs. Richard Glover."

"Where is this McCrae fellow? He all right?"

"He's a little *boy*," Anna said "A child. He's over there somewhere."

"You sure there wasn't nobody else with you?"

"No, that's all," Anna said.

"Now give me the addresses, please. Where did the nigger live?'

"For God's sake," Anna said. "What difference does it make? Go away and let me alone."

"I got to make my report, lady."

Ralph tugged at Anna's arm. "Mama, hadn't I better call Daddy?" he said.

"Yes," she said. "Yes, I guess you had." He has to find out, she thought. I can't put it off. Everybody has to find out that Estella is dead.

"Why doesn't the ambulance come with the resuscitator?" she asked the policeman. She was shivering uncontrollably.

"It's on the way," he said. "Now, these addresses . . ."

"She can't talk to you, Officer," someone behind her said. "She hardly knows what she's saying." Disembodied hands draped a big towel over her shoulders. "Here, Mrs. Glover, you're cold. Can I get you anything?"

She looked up. The white man who had brought them in was standing over her, dark curly hair falling on his high bony forehead, lips compressed by his effort at self-control. Deep lines grooved his face from the wings of his nose downward on either side of the mouth. Tenderness, strength, the knowledge of weakness, and pain had marked his face—it seemed a mask made to express her suffering.

"The ambulance," she said. "Tell them to hurry. There's still a chance . . ."

"I called them myself. They're on the way."

"Lady, I hate to keep worrying you," the policeman said, "but . . ."

"Officer . . ."

"Look, buddy, I got a job to do. I'm having a hard enough time getting anything out of her without you sticking your nose in it. Suppose you mind your own business."

"But he . . ." Anna began, and was shaken by a fit of shivering.

She heard a commotion on the levee. The steadily increasing crowd separated, and two white-jacketed men appeared and began to work over Estella. Behind them a woman with a camera snapped pictures.

"What are they taking *pictures* of her for?" Anna asked.

Then she heard her husband's voice shouting: "Get off the damn raft, goddamn it. Get off. You want to sink it? Get back there. You want to drown us all?"

The policeman stood up. "What the hell?"

"And put that camera up, if you don't want me to throw it in the lake." Richard Glover was in a fury of outrage, and concentrated it for the moment on the woman reporter from the local newspaper, who was snapping pictures of Estella.

"You all right, Anna?"

The people on the float were scuttling back to the levee, and the reporter had disappeared. Anna, who was still sitting where the policeman had left her, nodded and opened her mouth to speak, but her husband was gone before she could say anything. She felt a wave of self-pity. He didn't even stay to help me, she thought.

Then, a moment or an hour later—she did not know how long—she heard a strange, high-pitched shriek from the other end of the float. What's that, she thought. It sounded again—a long rasping rattle and then a shriek. Does the machine they brought make that queer noise?

"She's breathing," somebody said.

"No," Anna said aloud to nobody, for nobody was listening. "She's dead. I couldn't help it. I let her drown. Who's going to tell James?"

The float was cleared now. Besides Estella and Anna, only the two policemen, the two men from the ambulance, and Gaines Williamson were on it. The man who had rescued them was gone. The crowd stood quietly on the levee. In the doorway to the Yacht Club bar the reporter was talking to a third policeman.

"Where is Richard?" Anna said. "Did he leave?"

No one answered.

The long, rasping rattle and shriek sounded again. Gaines came over to where Anna was sitting and bent down to her, smiling kindly. "She's alive, Mrs. Glover," he said. "She's going to be all right."

Anna shook her head.

"Yes ma'am. She's moving and breathing, and yelling like crazy. She's going to be all right."

Anna got up shakily, feeling her knees buckle under her. She walked over to where the men were working Estella onto a stretcher.

"What's she doing?" she said. "What's the matter with her?"

Estella was thrashing her arms and legs furiously, mouth open, eyes staring, her face again the mask of mindless terror that Anna had seen in the lake. The rattle and shriek were her breathing and screaming.

"She must think she's still in the water," one of the men said. "Shock. But she's O.K. Look at her kick."

Anna sat down on the float, her knees giving way under her, and someone pulled her out of the way while four men carried the stretcher off the float and up the levee toward the ambulance.

Richard reappeared at the foot of the levee and crossed the walkway to the Yacht Club float. He bent down to help her up. "I'm sorry I had to leave you," he said. "I had to get the children away from here and find someone to take them home."

"She's alive, Richard," Anna said.

"Damn woman taking pictures," he said. "Damn ghoul. Newspapers!"

"She's alive," Anna said. "Somebody get me a drink. What I need is a drink."

Richard and one of the policemen got her on her feet and helped her up the levee to the car.

"My God," she said, "she's alive. They said she would be all right." And, in the car, "She kept pushing me down, Richard. I tried to hold her up. I tried to make her take hold of the boat. But she kept pushing me down."

"It's all right now," he said. "Try not to think about it any more."

IV

"IT'S A MIRACLE you didn't both drown," Carl Jensen said, when she had finished telling him her story.

One thing she had learned. "I wasn't afraid of the water," she said. "I didn't have sense enough to be afraid." She clasped her hands together nervously, felt a sharp stab of pain and looked down wonderingly at her fingers, bruised and swollen where they had been torn away from the hand grip on the skiff. "I knew I was a good swimmer," she said, "and I thought I was equal to anything. You remember what I told you Estella said after she killed the snake? 'There are times when you go down helpless in spite of all.' That's what I *didn't* know."

"You needn't take it all on yourself," he said. "You kept her from drowning."

"I suppose so," she said, and giggled. "I'm a heroine," she said. "Who would ever have thought I'd be a heroine?"

"But the lake," he said. "In a storm . . ." He broke off and then went on. "On a quiet, sunny day it's so peaceful you can't believe it's ever any other way, can you?" he said. He looked at the empty cigarette pack on the table beside him and absently searched his pockets for another pack while Anna watched him.

He was dressed as he had been the day of the accident in blue jeans and a tee shirt, his brown, muscular arms bare almost to the narrow shoulders, his thin body tense and lively as a coiled spring. She was struck again, as she had been when he had looked down at her on the dock, by the curious beauty of his face, a beauty not so much of flesh and feature as of line. He might have been born to be ugly or nondescript, a hill farmer with the downward lines of a life of heartbreaking toil, the sly, quick eyes of hatred and defeat; even his sexual power might have been transformed to the lust expressed in a salacious grin and satisfied in the cabins behind roadside taverns. Instead, it was as if by some miracle he had created himself from the raw materials of his life. His full lower lip curved gently upward in a shy smile, the thin upper lip lying sternly against it as if to deny the smile. His dark eyes under the high, bony brow looked out on the world with cautious intelligence, as if to say: Yes, I'm afraid to open the door, I'll admit. But I'll try. And the lines around his mouth! What had happened to make those marks?

Aloud she said, "Where did you disappear to the other day? Richard said he didn't see you at all, and the last time I remember seeing you was when you put the towel over my shoulders."

He was lighting the cigarette he had found in another crumpled pack in his pocket, and for a few minutes he did not answer. After he had put out the match, he held it in his hand, watching the smoke curl up, and then put it in an ashtray and looked at her hesitantly. She had for a moment the feeling that he might, after assessing her, get up and walk out without answering her question, and that she would then never see him again. But, with an effort, he began to speak of himself.

"I left," he said. "I got out." He was silent again.

"The policeman," she said. "I had forgotten."

"Yes," he said, "the policeman. I suppose I was afraid of him. Do you know what he said to me when he first came down and saw what had happened? '*Niggers!*' he said. 'These damn niggers! I wouldn't go out in a boat with one for all the money in the bank. And if I did, I sure wouldn't stick around to see what happened to him when the boat sank. One less, I'd say. So much the better. And then I'd take off. Unless I was aiming to kill myself.'" Jensen frowned at her as if she had spoken out in the policeman's behalf. "I know he sees too much," he said, "but . . ." He shrugged. "Did you look at him. Smooth and shining as an egg. Clean as a baby." He glanced at her half-defiantly, as if he had been told before that his point of view was womanish and, although he adhered to it stubbornly enough, expected her to reproach him.

"And then," he went on more confidently when she nodded, "you remember I yelled at the crowd on the dock to call an ambulance and get a resuscitator? And it didn't come for so long? Well, after about fifteen minutes, when it didn't come, I was going to call again to find out what had happened, and I began to ask the Negroes who had called and which hospital they had called, and, by God, they hadn't called anybody! 'Why not?' I said. 'Why the hell didn't you call anybody?' There must have been eight or ten of them standing on the dock when we pulled up, and not one . . . ! I was so mad, I was ready to fight them all. They looked at me. As blank as if they'd all just been baptized. 'Why not?' I said. And one of them says, 'Didn't none of us have a dime, boss, and it's a pay phone.' *Didn't none of us have a dime!*"

"Why do you reckon they didn't call?" Anna said.

He shook his head. "I've thought about it," he said. "The only thing I can figure out is maybe everyone thought someone else was doing it. That, or else they were all afraid if they called, they'd have to pay for the ambulance. If you send for one, you know, you have to give your name, and guarantee the fee. Maybe that was it."

Something in their situation as they sat smoking and talking so intimately in the little apartment, or perhaps it was something in her face—the still-dazed look of inward shock, the cloudy look in her eyes of pain and fear, as if she were slowly rising from deep anesthesia to the surface of consciousness—seemed to give him confidence.

"I began to get the feeling that I had a part in a play," he said. "Everything was too much itself. As if we'd been waiting in the wings for our cues—not the least of it being the curious way the wind brought the children's voices into my willow thicket." Again he smiled shyly. "Well," he said, "you can push that kind of thing too far. After all, I couldn't be sure how it was all meant to turn out. And when the policeman turned on me like that, it occurred to me that maybe after all the victim was to be, not the colored woman, but me. I'm afraid I have a leaning toward the victim's role. But that didn't seem to be the day for it. So I left."

"Yes," she said. "That's the way it was. And when I said a little while ago that I didn't know what I meant when I talked about it, I must have meant I wasn't sure yet what part I had played."

Before she left that afternoon he asked her if she intended to go out on the lake again, or if she had been frightened away for good.

"You can't give up the lake in the Delta," she said. "In the hills now, it would be different. Creeks and woods and ponds. But here there's nothing except the lake; everything else is cotton fields or swamp. And besides, I can't let the children get to be afraid of the water. It would make them miss too much." She broke off and blinked. Without warning she had seen her dream—Estella slipping off the side of the skiff, struggling, sinking. She moved her shoulders stiffly, as if to ease the pressure of a yoke fastened across them, and went on. "I'm still shaky," she said. "I think I'll wait a week or two before I go."

"If you'd like me to," he said, "I'll go out with you. I mean, I think it would help to have someone along the first time."

She almost said aloud the words in her mind: *Can* you help me? But instead answered calmly, "Thanks. I *would* like you to go. Richard's not much on fishing trips. But I want you to meet him, too." She nodded toward a pile of records and a record player on a table in the corner of the room. "I see you like music," she said. "So do we. You'll have to come out some night and eat supper with us and listen to records."

"I'm a sort of solitary bastard," he said.

"Well. We can all be solitary together."

And so it happened by degrees that Carl Jensen became an intimate of the Glover family. To begin with, it was a curious sort of intimacy, based at once on reserve and on openness. Richard Glover was a man who never failed to maintain the wall of privacy that makes human intercourse painless; he was almost incapable, outside his family, of giving confidences and, although he could do so if necessary, he had no desire to receive them. At the same time, his lively intelligence and wit and his interest in books, music, and human affairs in general (so long as they were not affairs personal to him) made him good company. In ten minutes' conversation he and Carl had learned that they could trust each other to keep their lives to themselves, and, reassured (Carl as much as Richard), they relaxed into friendship. The root of their liking for each other, aside from mutual trust and reserve, was music. Both were content to sit in silence for hours listening to Bach or Mozart, Scarlatti, Ravel, or Stravinsky. No apologies were necessary, no small talk had to interrupt. Carl even owned an alto recorder and had taught himself to read music, so that he could play all the lovely Renaissance and seventeenth-century airs. When Richard learned this, he dragged out a clarinet and insisted that Carl learn to play it. Before three months had passed the two men were playing chamber music together, Carl on the clarinet and Richard on oboe or piano.

These evenings together were a pleasure to Anna even though she could not, and had no desire to take part in the playing. She read or listened, got up and down to help her children with their homework and put them to bed. When the men stopped playing, the three of them sat and talked, covering the local gossip, or arguing good-naturedly about books and music, politics and art. There were no more than two or three other people in Philippi with whom the Glovers had so much in common.

It was not long before Anna began to see Carl in the daytime too. His hours at the radio station were irregular, and he was often free to join her and the children for picnics and fishing trips on the lake, and later in the year, when the weather was cold and rainy, for long drives through the gray, dissolving Delta countryside. Doubtless this intimacy furnished food for the Philippi gossips: the young bachelor, at least five years Anna's junior, the matron and her children, but never the husband. Neither Anna nor Richard was concerned. They never discussed the possibility of such gossip, and Anna did not know whether he had thought of it. She knew he was not jealous, and there was the end of the matter. That is not to say that she was not conscious of Carl Jensen as a man, for she was both conscious of him and attracted to him, and she knew he was attracted to her. But not by a word or a gesture did either of them violate the formal pattern of their friendship.

It would, however, have been strange if the friendship had not been intimate. Anna never lost the sense that they were bound to each other by mysterious bonds: the memory of his face, a mask of pain and pity bent down to her on the Yacht Club float, returned like her dream of Estella, as if it had been loosed in her mind from all the limiting circumstances of reality.

Their first time on the lake together was about two weeks after the accident. She did not take the children, for she wanted to be sure that she would not expose them to her fears. She had not known, when she decided to go, what she would feel, but she was filled with an unshakable determination to master herself, and so they set out. As soon as they had cast off and moved out into the deep water of the lake, beyond the sound of voices on the Yacht Club float, she was afraid. The day was sunny, but the water was dark. She wore a life jacket and had made Carl wear one, so that it would have been impossible for anything to happen to them in the water, but the fact of their physical safety made no difference to her fears. Looking down at the sparkling black surface of the lake, she marveled at her lost innocence. It was as if she had never known before that water had anything but a surface, that it was capable of doing anything but buoying her up. Now the surface was a curtain separating one order of reality from another. Chips of wood, matchsticks might bob and dance, water bugs might skate in safety, but below . . . She shivered and clutched the gunwales of the skiff with both hands, sitting stiffly in the bow, her life jacket buckled securely around her.

"I *will* get over it," she said to Carl. "It'll take time, but I will."

"Maybe getting over it is not what you need to do," he said. "Maybe you've got to get *with* it," he said. "You've got a new bed-fellow. You may not be able to shove him out."

"I've never gone at things that way," she said. But in truth she had already agreed with him, thinking as soon as he said, "You may not be able to shove him out," of Estella and what she had done with the death that had broken her life in two. Without having to think, she had shoved her unwelcome bedfellow out. She could not remember anything that had happened that day on the lake.

Richard, who had gone out to the hospital the night of the accident to see how she was getting along, had come home and told Anna that she was still out of her head. Every time she awakened, the screams and struggles began again. She was still in the lake and she stayed in it until late the following afternoon. For thirty hours she fought the black and yielding water, and then the magic in which she had put her faith came to her rescue. When the screams were worn to a whisper and the struggles to feeble convulsive movements of her arms and legs, that thirty hours vanished out of her life forever. In a puff of smoke from James's pipe, on a motey beam of late afternoon sun, the horror was consumed away. She woke up sane and quiet, knew her husband and grown daughter, and looked around the hospital room in amazement. She did not know why she was there.

The next day when Anna had come to call, they had told her about it. Estella recalled the picnic, and remembered getting into the skiff for the trip home, but everything after that was gone.

"James says you saved my life," she said to Anna in a hoarse whisper, "and I thank you."

James stood at the head of her bed, gray-haired and dignified in his Sunday suit. He nodded. "The day won't come when we'll forget it, Miss Anna," he said. "God be my witness."

Anna shook her head. "I never should have taken you out without a life preserver," she said.

"Ain't she suppose to be a grown woman?" James said. "She suppose to know better herself."

"How do you feel?" Anna asked.

"Lord, not a square inch on my body don't ache," Estella said. She laid her hands on the mound of her body under the sheet. "My stomach!" she said with a wry laugh. "Somebody must've jumped up and down on it."

"I reckon that's from the artificial respiration," Anna said. "I had never seen anyone do it that way before. They pick you up under the stomach and then put you down and lift your arms. And then, too, I kicked you. And we must have banged you up some getting you into the boat. Lord! The more I think about it, the worse it gets. Because Gaines hit you in the stomach, too, as soon as he got you into the boat. That's what really saved your life. I saw Gaines this morning," she said. "He cut his hands to shreds trying to get the fishing lines out of the screw, so he could get his boat going. And then as soon as he got you into the boat, he hit you in the stomach, and got rid of a lot of the water in your lungs and let in some air. I believe that breath you took in Gaines's boat kept you alive until we got you to the dock."

"You kicked me?" Estella said.

"When we were going down," Anna said, "and I finally knew I couldn't keep you up. I kicked you in the stomach and got loose from you, and then I grabbed you by the hair and held on, and about that time they saw us and the boats came. You passed out just when I kicked you, or else the kick knocked you out, because you didn't struggle any more. I reckon that was lucky, too."

So she told it at the time, and the kick was only an insignificant part of the story.

Estella shook her head. "I can't remember anything about it," she whispered. "Not anything." She pointed out the window toward the smokestack rising from the opposite wing of the hospital. "Seems like last night I got the idea there's a little man up there," she said. "He peeps out at me from behind that smokestack, and I'm afraid of him. He leans on the smokestack, and then he jumps away real quick, like it's hot, and one time he came right over here and stood on the window ledge and looked in at me. He wants to tell me something, yes, but he can't get in." She closed her eyes, seemed to drift off.

Anna looked anxiously at James.

"They still giving her something to keep her quiet," he said.

Estella opened her eyes. "I thank you, Miss Anna," she said. "James told me you saved my life." She smiled. "Seems like every once in a while I hear your voice," she said. "Way, way off. You're saying, 'I'll save you, Estella. Don't be afraid. I'll save you.' That's all I can remember."

Anna told Carl about her conversation with Estella. "I reckon you're right," she said. "I'd rather have this monster in the bed than on the window sill. But it's going to take time to get comfortable with him."

After that first expedition with Carl, Anna was absorbed in the act of taking in the revulsion she had felt that day. Again and again she took the children fishing, and at last the breach in her self-confidence began to be filled; practice enabled her to ignore the presence of darkness and death. Like a sailor who smokes habitually aboard a leaky oil tanker, although he knows one spark may blow him up, she began to be too bored with her own fears to care. But all the time this was happening, the dream returned, and she began to know as the months passed that it was a nightmare of failure, of cowardice. Estella's glassy eyes, turned on her at the moment of death, were saying: You won't help me. I know you'll let me die.

I could have hit her on the head with the paddle and knocked her out as soon as I knew the boat was sinking, she would say to herself, rehearsing what had happened for the hundredth time. And then: But I would never have done that. *Never.* Or she would think: If only I'd made her grab the Scotch cooler; it would have kept her up better than the skiff. And, facing the truth: It's nothing but an accident that she didn't die.

She wanted to speak of this to someone, *anyone,* but even more she wanted to hold on to her old knowledge of herself, to believe that once again, in time, everything would be all right.

During that queer fall and winter she clung to her new friendship with Carl as a distraction from herself, and drew him out to talk of his own life. He told her of his childhood, a past so foreign to Anna that at first she could not understand what he meant by the facts he gave her—bare stones of a reality altogether outside her experience.

For he had had, to begin with, nothing—no father, no mother, no love, no home, sometimes not even enough to eat or warm clothes. Only from the dim reaches of babyhood, recalled, like scenes on picture postcards, as firelight in a warm room or a face bending over him as a hand drew the covers up, could he remember his home and family. His father had deserted them when Carl was no more than four. Why—whether to go with someone else, or because he could not take care of them, or simply out of indifference—he never found out. Shortly afterwards his mother died, as he later learned, of septicemia after a miscarriage. His sister was adopted by an aunt and uncle; Carl was left to spend his childhood in the houses of one relative after another; poor people, with too many children of their own, who tolerated him only because they couldn't let him starve. When he told Anna about it, his hands trembled. "I took it for granted," he said, "that they adopted my sister because they loved her, and that no one adopted me because no one loved me." His voice was matter of fact. "Children take for granted such terrible things," he said.

And then, "I suppose they were good people, some of them. The ones who kept me, I mean. But it was the thirties. No one had any money. I don't remember that anyone was ever sorry to see me go. That sounds like self-pity, but it's true."

His grandparents he remembered with particular hatred, because his grandfather, a bearded old man with a face as sharp as an ax blade, talked so bitterly of his mother, calling her names like "Jezebel," and "Whore of Babylon," threatening his few precious memories of her kiss, her hand against his cheek; while his grandmother stood by, silent, grim, always in the act, it seemed, of stirring a pot or putting a steaming dish of greens on the table. He did not recall seeing his sister during those years. When he was fifteen someone told him that she had married and moved to California.

That was the year he began to educate himself, to read with almost mindless absorption every line of print he could lay his hands on, and it was then, too, that he first thought of looking for his father. Somehow in the school library he stumbled on the Russian novelists and read *Fathers and Sons* and *The Brothers Karamazov*. It was as if they spoke aloud to him, saying: Listen to us. We, too, have lived and suffered. We can help you.

He got a job making five dollars a week in a Jewish tailor's shop in the little town where he was living, paid two and a half board to his relatives to get out of some of his chores, and saved every cent of the rest. When he had saved a hundred dollars, he told himself, he would begin to look for his father, and he would not rest until he found him. Whether like Smerdyakov, to destroy him, or to hear him say like the poor old man Vasily Ivanovich, "Yevgeny, my son, my dear, my darling son!" he did not know; he only knew that he would set out. In truth, he dared not think of what would happen if he found his father, dared not hope, dared not allow himself to consider the possibility of failure, or worse, of reunion and then indifference.

"I don't think I really *thought* of anything all those years," he told Anna. "I can *see* people, how they walked, what they wore. I remember being miserable and even see myself being miserable, but not as if it were real, or I had understood any of it—more as if it were a queer, unhappy dream that lasted for years."

He looked for his father a long time, long at least for a lad of sixteen, nearly a year. He husbanded his money, hitchhiking from town to town and stopping occasionally to work a week or two to make it last longer. He made a plan and carried it out in town after town all through Mississippi, Louisiana, Tennessee, and Arkansas. He would stop at a town and go to the second- and third-rate hotels and flophouses, asking the desk clerks if anyone by the name of Carl Jensen had ever registered with them, asking permission to look through their old registers. He knew his father had been a salesman, and in cities like New Orleans and Memphis he would go to all the places that hired men to sell things like can openers and vacuum cleaners, and ask if they had ever had a salesman named Jensen. "Of course, it was all crazy," he told Anna. "Why should he have stayed in the South? He might just as well have been in California or Minnesota as in Arkansas. But I suppose I must have thought when I finished with the South I would move on to other parts of the country. It never occurred to me that I would stop before I found him.

"Sometimes," he said, "I would see him. Can you imagine that? I didn't even remember what he looked like, but I would see someone walking down the street ahead of me and I would know, I would be *sure* it was my father. Two or three times I stopped people and asked them their names. And worse was to be walking in a crowd and think: You, or you, any of you might be him; to be haunted by the notion that he might be sitting next to me at the counter in a café, that like two ghosts we might drift past each other again and again without seeing each other."

In November of 1944, when he had been looking for his father for nearly a year, he contracted pneumonia. He scarcely knew he was ill. Vaguely he recognized that the heat of his body, the tightness in his chest were unusual. But he had been in a fever for years, and every muscle of his body was accustomed to the cramping tightness of anxiety. He followed his schedule as usual, sitting one night in a fifty-cent-a-night flophouse in a small town in northern Mississippi with a blanket draped around his shaking shoulders, mapping out his plan for the following day. Next morning, like a sleepwalker, he got up, walked to the outskirts of the town, and began to thumb a ride. He stood for an hour or more in the cold November wind before someone picked him up—a farmer who turned off the highway onto a dirt track fifteen miles from the nearest town, and left him there. He had no more luck that day. He had forgotten to eat breakfast and he had had no lunch. Alternately walking and waiting, he managed to go five miles before he collapsed in the neat, broom-marked yard of a small Negro cabin by a crossroad. His last sane memory was of an old woman looking down at him in exasperation and saying, "Get up, white boy. Can't you see I ain't able to lift you? You want to lay out here and freeze?"

"Yes," he said.

A gust of wind blew dust and leaves across his face and he ground the grit between his teeth in a fit of shaking.

"She took me in," he told Anna, "and nursed me for weeks. I don't remember much about it, but I must have told her I didn't have any family, that there was no one to notify. I had two dollars in my pocket—all that was left of the money I had saved and what I had

earned working off and on that year. She didn't seem to care, to be interested in money one way or the other, although I found out afterwards that she had several hundred dollars in the house, hidden under the paper on the kitchen wall.

"I remember one crazy thing that first day when she had gotten me into the house in spite of myself and was trying to get me into bed. All I wanted was to be going—if I couldn't die—to be moving on. I kept looking down at my legs, saying 'Walk! Walk!' and they wouldn't. She didn't pay any attention to that, but pulled off my jacket, and I remember I curled my toes down against the soles of my shoes to hold them on, because I knew if she got my shoes, I'd be lost. 'Leggo your shoes, white boy,' she said. 'You want to get my sheets dirty?' 'Not getting in your bed,' I said. 'Thank you. I got to go.' And I seemed to be walking again. I walked into my grandfather's kitchen. I thought my father was there. I was sure I heard his voice. But instead, there were my grandfather and grandmother. She was bending over the stove, and her hair was steamy—hanging down around her face in wet ropes. There were greens cooking, and God knows what else—three or four steaming pots. And he—my grandfather—was covered with hair, his face, everything. His beard had grown down to his feet. I was terrified and I ran. All I could think of was to run. And someone kept holding my feet, trying to take my shoes.

"She pulled them off—strong for an old woman—and gave me a shove into bed, and I can see her standing over me, her face brown and wrinkled up and squinty and her mouth too full of teeth, like a little old monkey. The walls were papered with newspapers, the headlines cartwheeling around her head.

"'What do you want with me?' I said. 'I'm nobody. You understand? Nobody.'

"She said, 'It is written, *If thine enemy hunger, feed him.*'

"'I want my shoes,' I said.

"'I'll keep your shoes for you and give them back,' she said, and I saw she had them in her hand. She put them on the floor by the bed, and put her hand on my forehead. 'Go to sleep, white boy,' she said. 'I'll take care of you. You are my brother.'

"'My name is Carl Jensen,' I said, 'and I am not your brother.'

"'We are our Father's children,' she said.

"After that, I don't remember anything for quite a while. She took care of me three weeks or more before I knew what was going on. When I began to be well, I stayed on there, doing chores, chopping wood, working in her garden. She was so old and feeble, I don't know where she found the strength that first day, and then afterwards, to take care of me. And she was alone. She had two grown nephews who lived in the next town down the road, but they never came to see her. That suited me. I didn't want to see anyone or be seen by anyone. I hadn't the strength to move on or make a decision, and I knew if anyone saw me there, I would have to decide to do something. If anyone passed by (and once in a while one of her neighbors who lived a little way down the road or the white man who owned the place would stop to see her), I hid. I worked and ate and slept and never let myself be seen by anyone but her all that time. Isn't that queer? But it's true. I stayed hidden almost three months. She didn't question it. I don't think she had ever questioned the act of any human being in her life. She never said another word about God, never asked where I had come from, never wondered what I was going to do. We got along fine. After all, I had been raised on farms. I knew what had to be done and did it. And when night came, we were both so tired, she from age and I from weakness, we slept like the dead. After I was well enough to know what was going on, I got her to fix me a pallet and slept on the floor by the fire in the front room, and she slept on her bed. She had been sleeping in a chair while I was sick.

"I wasn't crazy any more. I never thought again about looking for my father, just sometimes saw myself as I had been, remembered my obsession, and wondered what I could have thought would come of it. It was as if I had become another person. I knew I had to begin to live, and I stayed there, waiting for the strength to do it.

"I saw, too, that she needed me. Maybe she went down during the time I was sick, maybe it was the last strength she had that she gave me, but I didn't see how, old and weak as she was, she had been making out by herself. By the time two months had passed, I was beginning to turn over in my mind what to do about her, how she was going to live when I left. I tried to talk to her about it, but she wouldn't. 'Ne' mind,' she would say. 'I taken care of myself before you come.'

"She died in her sleep one night without a sound. No one had seen me come, no one knew I was there, and so I left. I laid her out straight in the bed like you read in books you are supposed to do, and put the cover up to her chin. I couldn't bear to cover her face, although I thought to myself that you were supposed to do that, too. I took the money out from behind the newspaper on the wall where she had showed me she kept it, and put it in a chest, so someone would find it. Then I started off walking down the road. I couldn't be grieved for her. In fact, I felt a kind of joy—do you know what I mean? The joy that comes with the death of old people, as if such a death makes you feel to the very bone of your soul the mystery and heroism of a human life.

"I stopped at the first cabin I came to, about a mile and a half down the road, and made up a story about having stopped to ask for a drink of water and found the old woman dead, and then I walked on."

They were sitting on a blanket under a sycamore tree on the big sandbar at the south end of the lake when he told her this last story, one soft day in April of the year following the accident. The lake was high, full of the roiled and muddy water of the spring rise, the sky clear, the greening willows and furry young cottonwood leaves delicately fresh. As he talked, she had felt the tremor of impact, as if an ax were thudding against the joists and pillars of her life. For a few minutes, after he finished, she was silent. Then, "Is that all?" she said.

He nodded.

She picked up a stick and began to draw in the firm damp sand the outline of a house, its roof sagging on one side, its doors and windows knocked awry. Then, still absorbed, she rubbed it out and spoke again, the self-conscious irony of accepted failure in her face and voice.

"That's all very well for you, and for *her,*" she said. To herself she added, "But I kicked Estella away." She shrugged her shoulders and brushed furiously at the sand on her hands and legs, brushing off, as it were, an uncompleted part of herself, the imagined but always possible heroisms of childhood, now removed forever from her reach. Then she smiled at him and got up. "It's late," she said. "We'd better be getting home."

When they tied up at the Yacht Club float, the April evening was drawing in. Beyond the quiet waters of Lake Okatukla, the willow trees were misted with green. The sun had set in a cloudless sky, the fires of evening had died, and the world was filled with the dark blue radiance of twilight. Small waves lapped at the float and hissed and whispered against the concrete pavement of the levee. Carl picked up their lunch basket.

As he and Anna crossed the float toward the levee, they heard the faint sound of someone singing:

"No, no, no, no, no,
I thought you cared,
But now I know
Hearts are made of stone . . ."

"That's Estella," Anna said. "Look, Carl, there she is, on the terminal walkway."

In the clear dying light they saw her. She had stopped fishing and was standing on the walkway rolling her line around her pole. The breeze lifted her loose dress away from the strong columns of her legs, and the last rays of blue twilight lit her golden face. She finished winding the line around her pole and stood looking into the west, still singing, like an incantation to the gathering dusk: "No, no, no, no, no . . ."

"Come on," Anna said. "We can give her a ride home."

They started together across the levee near the water's edge, and halfway to the terminal he touched her on the shoulder.

"Anna?"

"Hmmm?"

"What I meant was . . ." He broke off. "Are you all right?" he said.

"I'm still trying," she said in a low voice and then, aloud, calling through the dusk, across the distance between them, "Estella? Hey, Estella."

"Miss Anna? Is that you?"

"Come on down and join us," Anna said.

Afterword
by Ellen Douglas

During the late nineteen fifties and early sixties I spent my time chasing three rambunctious boys, writing the stories in *Black Cloud, White Cloud,* and putting together my first novel, *A Family's Affairs.* I would work on the novel in the winter when my children were in school and on the stories in the summer when, between fishing trips and expeditions to the Indian mounds and baseball games, I occasionally had a few hours alone—although seldom the unbroken stretch of time necessary to sustain the ongoing momentum of a novel.

The character Anna in *Black Cloud, White Cloud* is of course the same Anna who is the maturing child in *A Family's Affairs.* The novel explores the lives of the grown people by whom Anna is surrounded and formed—her family's lives. More central to the stories are the moral dilemmas posed for the child and young woman living among black people in the South: An old black woman stands in a doorway maintaining order at a children's party. How did she come to be here, living with a white family, and what might be the consequences for her and for the people with whom she has lived? A white woman talks compulsively of the foibles of her black servant.

Is that guilt in her voice or does she scarcely seem to understand what she is saying? A child swims away from an overturned skiff into the path of a towboat and his mother opens her mouth to call him back, while the body of a drowned woman bumps at her legs. What is to be done?

I knew these people, heard them speak, recognized as my own the predicaments they grappled with, and cobbled up stories to make them live. One story and then another and another. For how could I, living in this time and place, fail to write about these lives—about the corrosive hatreds, the crippled loves, the confusions, the flashes of nobility and heroism, the ways of making do, making room?

But I did not, when I first began writing the stories, think of them as a book, and I remember vividly how one summer night the book came together for me. The year must have been nineteen sixty-one. The separate black and white societies of the South and the country were grinding against each other with the agonized crunch of continental plates, preparing the earthquakes and volcanic eruptions of the sixties. The Old Miss riot would follow in sixty-two, Freedom Summer with its murders and bombings and church burnings in sixty-four. I had finished "Hold On"—it was published that year in a shortened version in *The New Yorker*—and was rewriting "The House on the Bluff," which I had begun some years earlier. The other stories didn't yet exist except as shadows across my life.

My husband and I were listening that summer night to the Virgil Thomson settings of a group of William Blake's poems. I remember how the music intensified the feeling of the poems for me almost unbearably: the soaring beauty of "Mercy, Pity, Peace and Love," the drumbeat and clash of rolled cymbals in "Tyger, Tyger," and, in "The Little Black Boy," the *sung* lines, "I'll shade him from the heat till he can bear/To lean in joy upon our Father's knee," and the terrible complex irony and tragedy of that final falling line, "And be like him, and he will *then* love me." I said to myself: This song is about what my stories are about and I have others, not yet written, to go with them. This is a book and I want to find the title in this poem and to use the poem as an epigraph. And so I did.

I continued in all my later books to write about the complexities of family ties and the lives, cheek by jowl, in bed and out, in and out of the ditch, of blacks and whites. But now, rereading the whole of *Black Cloud, White Cloud* for the first time in many years, I see that other concerns also found their first expression in the two early books. Although I may have meant to set out with each book on a new exploration (This one, I hear myself say, is entirely different), it's apparent that old preoccupations, old loves and hates have surfaced again and again.

Already in *A Family's Affairs*, when Anna is telling stories of which she is the heroine while somebody else plays second fiddle, I had begun to think about the nature of story telling—lives as stories and the relation of stories to truth. And in "The House on the Bluff," when Caroline writes to Anna, "Did you ever think that stories have happy endings? Well, they don't. No, there is no form to them . . . everything is confusion," the story at some level seems to ask: Is this true? Don't lives shape themselves like stories? Or, aren't stories imitations of the shapes of lives? In "Hold On," Anna sees the way people "play the part of themselves" and resolves to remember *the truth*, not a made-up story that transforms her into a heroine. Again, in "Jesse," there is the device of having Anna *forced* to listen, so that the inner story comes, as it seems, not from the author, but from Jesse himself. These are concerns I returned to in *A Lifetime Burning* and approached through the patterns of myth and fairy tale in *The Rock Cried Out* and *Can't Quit You, Baby*.

Then there is water. How could my work not be shaped by water? I have lived my whole life on rivers—on the Mississippi, the Red, again on the Mississippi, and now on what's left of the Pearl. As a child I used to say that when I died I wanted to be put in a hollow log like DeSoto, weighted with chains and dropped into the river. Now, reading in "On the Bluff," "Anna, like a skater on cracking ice, saw the surface of the Bairds' life broken and for a moment glimpsed unimagined and threatening depths," and, in "Hold On," the descriptions of the surface and depths of the lake, I recall the metaphors of the breaking dam in *The Rock Cried Out* and the waterskier in *Can't Quit You, Baby.* Of course, when I thought of using the dam and skier, I'd forgotten both the skater and the almost-drowning of the earlier books. But water has flowed through all my books, offered itself to be put to use in all sorts of circumstances: springs, ponds, bayous, creeks, lakes, rivers; sand bars, bluffs, levees, dams; and for our human use, skis and skiffs, ferries, towboats, and fishing poles.

On land—for our human use, and as witness to the lives of the people in them—there are houses, created and furnished almost without thought in *A Family's Affairs,* more consciously in "The House on the Bluff," again in *Where the Dreams Cross, Apostles of Light, The Rock Cried Out,* and *A Lifetime Burning.* Women, of course, take care of houses. Writing about them seems a natural passion for a middle-class female writer of my generation—a generation of women who mostly stayed at home raising children, polishing silver, cooking meals, digging in their gardens—taking care of their houses.

Now, though, looking back, I have a curious sense that I have camped out in my life, lived not in a house but in a metaphorical tent, that a writer's work is her house and can be carried from one place to another as if in a back pack. I see myself, instead, in the wilderness or, like the children in *The Scotch Twins* (a book I loved at nine and ten), hiding from outlaws in a cave behind a waterfall.

What seems most intense to me in "The House on the Bluff"— the children's sense of a wilderness world beyond the orderly confines, the brick-walled borders of their lives—fades, I think, in the later books. I feel its presence in the garden scenes in *Apostles of Light* and in the young hero Alan's fantasies as he wanders the woods in *The Rock Cried Out*—a nostalgia for a vanished world, threatening yet beloved, both plunged into and held at bay. But then, like the patches of real wilderness remembered from my childhood, even the fantasy vanishes. Perhaps it's no longer useful to me, no longer has the power it once had to evoke passion. Like the canalized river in *A Lifetime Burning,* trapped by locks, flowing first one way and then the other, it is changed, tamed—no, not tamed—violated, murdered.

But then, everything has changed. Houses that used to be "down at the heel" have been restored and are listed on the National Register of Historic Places. Black women don't live as servants with white families: the confrontation with ambiguous authority that informs "The House on the Bluff" is as irrelevant to the lives of adolescents these days as the fate of all those doomed nineteenth century heroines who committed adultery or bore children out of wedlock. Black musicians like Jesse, instead of enduring the guilty condescension of white employers, play to sell-out crowds in Paris and Tokyo. If they're canny and fortunate, they may even manage to collect their record royalties. The real boy whose fictional counterpart swam away from the boat in "Hold On" serves now in the state legislature, and a black man of his generation, who grew up as he did in a small Mississippi river town, serves in the Congress of the United States. Carrie Lee's granddaughter may soon be mayor of a Delta town.

But no matter the dizzying change in mores, no matter that I, who wrote these stories, can scarcely manage to dredge up from my memory the look of streets and farms and creeks and woods in that lost world, some realities stay with us, and writers of fiction continue to explore them. Stories and truth pull against each other in their ancient tug of war. Water flows through all our dreams. Houses shelter and reject us and record our passage. And human poverty and suffering still bear a racial stamp. It is still necessary to say with Anna, "Do we expect by our confession miraculously to relieve the suffering of the innocent?" And with Carrie Lee, "If you wants to play, you gits on in there and eats they pudding."

This volume was designed by John A. Langston. The text was set in 10½ point Linotron Sabon with display in 24 point Sabon by G&S Typesetters Inc. of Austin, Texas. It was printed and bound by The Murray Printing Company of Westford, Massachusetts.